Stonewall Inn Mysteries
Keith Kahla, General Editor

One Dead Drag Queen

A Tom & Scott Mystery

MARK RICHARD ZURBO

ST. MARTIN'S PRESS ✳ NEW YORK

www.stonewallinn.com

Library of Congress Cataloging-in-Publication Data

Zurbo, Mark Richard.
    One dead drag queen / Mark Richard Zurbo.
        p. cm.
    "The Tom and Scott mysteries"–p. i.
    ISBN 0-312-20937-1 (hc)
    ISBN 0-312-27702-4 (pbk)
    Carpenter, Scott (Fictitious character)–Fiction. 2. Mason, Tom (Fictitious character)–Fiction. 3. High School teachers–Fiction. 4. Baseball players–Fiction. 5. Chicago (Ill.)–Fiction. 6. Gay men–Fiction. I. Title.

PS3576.U225 054 2000
813'.54–dc21   00–029674

First Stonewall Inn Mysteries edition: July 2001

10 9 8 7 6 5 4 3 2 1

For Ric Carlson—for courage and hope

For Paul Varnell—for chocolate and companionship

One
Dead
Drag Queen

.1.

The death threats had started in June of last year. The number of anonymous phone calls and threatening letters had increased week by week, and a tap on the phone had done no good. Calls from pay phones, calls from area codes not hooked up for caller-ID tracing, calls using the caller-ID block, all very untraceable. Finally, after changing our phone number three times, we got a service to screen our calls. Everyone, including our parents, has to go through the service. Twice someone had broken into the phone company's computer system and gotten the direct number. I had answered the phone both times. Even though I'd slammed the receiver down as soon as the obscenities started, it was never fast enough to stop the motes of terror from trembling at the edge of consciousness. Every time the phone rings now, I hesitate. Is this the time it's going to be some lunatic who's going to try going beyond threats?

All our mail is screened through metal detectors. Any

packages not sent by someone we know are dealt with by bomb experts.

My paranoia had grown so much that I'd hired a security firm for the times when I make public appearances. They prevented any major attacks, but they weren't able to stop the excess of minor annoyances. I'm not sure anyone could. There are just too many crazies in the world.

A doorman at the penthouse, an alarm system at Tom's place—I thought they would be enough, at least enough against an individual madman. Even I didn't expect a terrorist attack.

Tom says it a lot, that he'd never live in fear, but that's all we've done lately. Live in fear.

Complicating all this is that Tom is a worrier by nature. He's good at it too. Even if nothing is going wrong, he can dredge up obscure problems to brood and fret over. What's worse is that lately I've caught the worry bug from him.

Until that Saturday, I always figured I was the one in the most danger. My memories of the early part of the day are very clear.

I cleaned all morning. Yeah, I have a maid service come in, but there's just a whole lot of clutter and personal mess that I attend to. And I like to go around to all the rooms and put on the finishing touches. Tom is reasonably good about being tidy. His attention to detail doesn't match my standards, but he's much better than he used to be. Still, I wish he helped with the cleaning more than he does. That man sheds enough hair of a morning in a bathroom to start his own fur farm—the price for having a furry-chested lover. Tom once said that I was obsessive-compulsive about cleaning. I admit neatness is important to me, but he doesn't use that phrase anymore. Not after a fight we had seven years ago, which began with him using that phrase. At the time I felt compelled to remind him of several of his failings. We compromised. I eased up on him. He cleaned more.

That morning, Tom left at seven. He'd volunteered to help with the office work for a friend of his at the Human Services Clinic. I did a light workout and then began doing chores.

When I clean, I play annoying country music. Loudly. Loud enough to be heard in Indiana, maybe. When Tom's out of the house, I can play the kind of music I grew up with, but which he hates. I also sing along with the music. Loudly. I confine my singing to the privacy of my own home. Tom says this is a good thing.

It took less than an hour to finish all the bathrooms and the kitchen. After a couple loads of laundry, a little dusting and light vacuuming, I was onto the fourth repeat of the new Garth Brooks CD and ready for lunch.

The afternoon was great. I had been looking forward to spending the time working on a rocking chair I'd been building. I'd started making it several weeks ago. It's going to take months to finish. Solid oak. Precise measurements. No music now. Just silence. The smell of wood—newly sawn and freshly sanded. Studying plans. My hands touching, eyes judging. Adding individual touches such as minute carved figures in the sides of the arms and runners. I'd learned carpentry and carving from my granddad during long summer twilights in the old barn on his farm down the road from my folks' place. The rocker was for my parents' fiftieth wedding anniversary. Mostly of an evening they sit on the porch on their farm in Georgia rocking and listening to the insects. The joy, tedium, and precision involved in such a project erase all thoughts of time as I immerse myself in creating.

I finished sanding the left runner about six. I shut my eyes and slowly caressed the newly worked bare wood. I opened

3

my eyes, leaned back against my workbench, and enjoyed the pleasurable exhaustion I get when I've worked hard, and I can see and feel my own handiwork taking shape.

I wondered if I should clean up before Tom got home. He was a little late, but when he'd left, he'd said he wasn't sure how long it would take. We didn't have firm dinner plans. I wasn't in the mood to go out. I was ready for a quiet evening at home.

I finished my shower just as the broadcast of the late-Saturday-afternoon college football game should have been ending. Instead, WBBM, the CBS affiliate in Chicago, was showing a special news report. A street scene. The reporter standing directly in front of a slew of emergency vehicles. Rotating lights in the immediate background. Farther behind, flames gushed from the front of a building. I recognized the local reporter, Brandon Kearn. He worked for MCT, Metro Chicago Television, which was started five years ago to rival CLTV as a local news source. Kearn was as famous for his good looks as he was for his legendary salary negotiations—he was by far the highest-paid reporter in the city. I wondered why he was on CBS and what part of Chicago had caught fire this time. I reached for the remote to change the channel. Just because another building is burning doesn't mean I've got to watch. Nor did I want to see the unfortunate victims or inarticulate bystanders being interviewed live.

But I couldn't find the damn TV remote. Why Tom can't put it back in the same place every time, I don't know.

Kearn was saying, ". . . ripped apart most of this city block fifteen minutes ago. There are six people confirmed dead. There are believed to be numerous victims still in the rubble. The fire department is working frantically to keep the blaze from spreading so possible survivors can be rescued from under the debris. It doesn't look good."

I found the remote under the seat cushion where it had slipped the night before as I was watching TV. My fault this time.

My hand froze on the controls as Kearn continued, "The Human Services Clinic was among the buildings almost completely obliterated."

▴ 2 ▴

My memories of the rest of that night come back to me in disconnected flashes. I know I peered closely at the street scene behind the reporter. I recognized nothing. It was late and the clinic must have been closed. Probably everyone had left.

The phone rang.

Queasiness burbled in my stomach. A crazed computer hacker with a hate-on for us, or Tom calling to reassure me? The woman at the answering service said, "You have an urgent call." She gave me the number. It was a 773 area code, which meant it was anywhere in the city of Chicago outside the Loop.

I tapped in the numbers. It rang seven times before someone answered.

I didn't recognize the voice. I said who I was. The other person said, "This is Gloria Dellios. I work with Tom Mason at the Human Services Clinic. There's been an explosion."

"How is Tom?"

"No one has seen him. They think he's trapped under the rubble. I'm sorry. They've pulled out a number of people alive. There's still hope."

I don't remember hanging up the phone. I barely remember throwing on socks, jeans, shoes, and a sweatshirt, then grabbing my wallet and car keys. I remember wiping away tears as I took the elevator to the ground floor. Outside, it was a cloudless, crisp, perfect October evening.

I recall running several red lights on Michigan Avenue and not caring who beeped and cursed. I remember thinking about losing Tom and being without him for the rest of my life. I know I thought about all the things we wouldn't be able to do together. I guess it sounds sappy, but I remember thinking it was too perfect a day for Tom to die. Maybe some of this sounds like cheap sentiment, but I don't care. Tom knows how to use words—he's the English teacher, not me— and Tom always says he loves cheap sentiment. That Dickens made a career out of it. I've never read Dickens. I just know I love Tom.

The Human Services Clinic wasn't one building. It had started in a three-story former home on the northwest corner and had gradually expanded over the years to encompass all the buildings on the North Side of Fulton all the way from Racine to Elizabeth. Most of the buildings were over a century old.

I took Grand Avenue over the Chicago River and turned south on Racine. Maybe the trip took ten minutes. Maybe five. I couldn't get within four blocks of the place. Parking on the near west and north sides of Chicago is hellish at the best of times. I found an empty spot in a little parking lot under the el tracks. The clinic paid to have these few spaces at a distance from the entrance as a staging ground for patients to be escorted from. I saw Tom's truck parked next to one of the struts supporting the el. As I got out of my car, a train rumbled by overhead. The cacophony it made was unable to drown out the screaming sirens still approaching the scene.

My first impression was of people frantically rushing about. Firemen, paramedics, and cops swarmed over the area. They were far outnumbered by the injured and the passersby giving assistance to them. People dripping blood were being carried away from the scene. The ambulatory were gently escorted to a triage area to await their turn. Sitting at a curb was a woman with a gash across her forehead. She held a weeping child.

I saw someone on a stretcher being wheeled up to a waiting ambulance. I hurried to get as close as I could. It was a black woman. I stopped a guy in fire gear to try to get information.

He said, "Nobody knows anything definite."

"My lover was working in the clinic today."

"I'm sorry, buddy." He tried to pull out of my grasp.

I held on to his arm. "Who would know if he'd gotten out?"

"I don't know who could tell you. I gotta go."

"What if he's in there? Are they going to be able to stop the fire?"

"There's a chance." The fireman pointed. "The fire's at the far end of the block near Carroll Street. They're doing everything they can to stop the spread." I let him go.

I got as close as I could to the destruction. I was on Fulton Street halfway between Racine and Elizabeth. The entire city block from Carroll to Fulton and Racine to Elizabeth had been nearly obliterated. Masses of debris, great heaps of rubble, shattered glass, innumerable fragments of people's lives, were scattered between me and the center core of devastation. To the east of the devastated block across Racine

Street, several buildings, including the new Health and Fitness Forever Club, had been severely damaged.

Rescue workers swarmed over the building remnants at the end of the block near me. Few glanced at the approaching flames. In the street nearby, every few moments someone would rush about bringing injured from the scene or toting stretchers to it.

No one stood and stared at the devastation. No one told me to go away. I moved forward to help.

Rotating lights, flames inching closer, car and truck headlights, orange streetlights, burnt-out cars. It felt and looked wickedly strange. I'd dropped Tom off at the clinic several times, but I was even more familiar with the neighborhood from the deli we stopped at once in a while on Carroll Street. Mr. and Mrs. Fattatuchi served the best chicken salad in the city. Flames were already past where their restaurant had been. They were a sweet old couple. Saturday night was the busiest of the week for them. They would have been inside when the explosion came.

The block had been a mix of upscale urban renewal projects next to three- and four-story buildings long past the need for a wrecking ball. Like the clinic complex, many of these were over a hundred years old. Many were caught in a lawsuit between preservationists and developers. That suit would be moot now. Lots of these buildings were "residential hotels," a synonym often used in more polite circles to describe a flophouse. The newer buildings had brightly lit, glass-fronted, trendy retail stores in first floors, mostly offices and a few lofts on the floors above.

Along the block, between the fire and me, parts of interiors and a few exterior walls still stood. For the one hundred yards nearest to me, not much remained above two feet high. I wondered how anyone had gotten out alive.

10

The Human Services Clinic had been a focal point for protesters for years. The clinic gave prenatal care and family planning counseling as well as performing abortions. If it was a slow news day, the local press could count on at least a few people from one or both sides in the controversy being in front of the building. Usually there were a couple bored cops making sure the two sides kept apart. Quite a while back when the picketing had started, the demonstrations had become violent, but I didn't remember hearing anything in that vein for a long time.

They didn't let Tom work out front where the women came in. Some of the clientele and a few of the employees were pretty hostile to the presence of men. That was okay with Tom. He worked in the basement. Filing, typing, stuffing envelopes.

A woman approached me. Her blue jeans were torn. One sleeve of her white shirt was ripped off at the shoulder. A large bandage covered that arm from wrist to elbow. The remnant of the shirt was covered with grime and dirt.

"Scott Carpenter?"

I was wary as I always seemed to be of strangers these days. "Yeah?"

"I'm Gloria Dellios. I recognize you from your pictures in the media."

"Is Tom all right?"

"I'm sorry, I don't know." She pointed halfway down the block. "There's an alley down there. Debris was blown from that point outward in all directions. There's a huge crater in the ground. The clinic was at this end of the block. I was on the steps walking out when the explosion happened. I was lucky, I was in front of one of the stone pillars. Still I was thrown halfway across the street. I'm afraid Tom was working in the back, about a third of the way down the block from the explosion."

I felt tears.

"The fire isn't near there yet. It started on the south side of Carroll Street. They've pulled out eight survivors from the clinic so far, so there's still hope."

A bulldozer lumbered up to the entrance of the alley. I figured they were trying to move the debris to create a fire-break. At the moment it looked as if it might not be necessary. Water cascaded from four different hoses between the fire and this half of the block. At this point I could barely see any flames.

"Is there anyone who knows anything definite?" I asked.

"I'm not sure anyone would really have information beyond what we can see. Everybody's concentrating on stopping the fire and getting people out first, then they'll start investigating."

I hated the reasonableness of her words.

I found a group of people clearing debris near where I thought Tom might have been working. Twenty feet away, a line of ambulances moved almost continuously as victims were hurried inside. I wanted to stay close to the medical personnel. Where they worked was the most likely spot to bring Tom when they found him.

I wondered how they would be able to discern any desperate voice through the frantic sounds of the emergency vehicles. The innumerable fire personnel were forced to add to the noise and confusion as they performed their essential tasks.

All I remember of the next half an hour is chaos unimaginable. Heat and flames. Water and smoke. Shouts and cries. Fire hoses and darkness. Jury-rigged lights swaying from wobbly poles. A man and woman sobbing loudly hurrying past, followed closely by a camera crew. I remember thinking the damn reporters could cease their inanity for a minute and do something really important, like help. The mostly silent workers around me only occasionally stopped to stare at the slowly abating conflagration. Periodically a gentle breeze floated in from the lake carrying heavy white smoke drifting in our direction.

Once a guy next to me said, "Aren't you Scott Carpenter, the baseball player?"

I didn't deny it. He shrugged and we both kept working.

Fifteen minutes later the fire was two buildings away from the alley, but it was obvious that its progress was almost completely checked.

They hadn't found anyone under the debris in quite a while.

Dellios found me again. "We're setting up an area for the families and friends."

"I'm going to stay here and help," I said.

Brandon Kearn and his camera crew rushed up. They crowded toward me. Kearn spoke into the camera, "We have learned that the controversial baseball player Scott Carpenter is present at the scene." Because I'd come out as an active, openly gay baseball player, I was often referred to as controversial. I seldom felt controversial. More like I was the normal one and the rest of them needed to catch up. I was not in the mood to be harassed.

Kearn was around thirty, tall, with wavy, black hair, and golden brown skin. I'd met him. He was generally more sensitive and more sensible than most reporters. Then again this was probably the story of a lifetime for him.

Kearn shoved the microphone toward me. "What can you tell us about the explosion?"

I exercised my right to remain silent, my right to be more

13

concerned with my lover, and my right to turn my back and keep working. They gave up on me and rushed to another instance of disaster and death for more exploitation of those in pain. That all those around me and everyone in the television audience now knew I was there only added to my dislike of sensationalistic journalism.

Several moments later, a man standing near the edge of the clinic debris shouted. He waved frantically, and along with other rescue workers I rushed to him. People concentrated on hurling debris away from a central spot. I joined the others in picking up items and passing them to the person behind me in line. In front of me I saw a rescue worker holding a hand. It had a wedding ring on it. Not Tom. Five minutes later, they eased a woman out of the mess—I couldn't tell if she was breathing—and rushed her over to the paramedics. Seconds later she was lost to my sight.

At no point did anyone say go away. No cops tried to keep only official people present. Mostly we sifted through debris and listened.

After uncounted minutes of mindless effort, I glanced at the fire. I could no longer see any flickers of blue, red, orange, or yellow. Billowing clouds of smoke did continue, often causing us to stoop as close to the ground as possible. It looked as if this part of the destruction would be spared the flames. If Tom was alive—the most horrible "if" I ever wanted to face—if he was alive, we'd be able to get to him.

A glance at the perimeter of the scene showed that some degree of order was being brought to the search. Personnel with bullhorns at their sides were being given orders from a central point. I saw five top-level police officers conferring about fifty feet to the right. The firefighters seemed to be working with well-coordinated efficiency.

Then there was a large yellow flash followed by a deafening boom.

14

3

I found myself on the ground. Only a few seconds seemed to have passed. My ears rang and I could vaguely hear shouts around me. I shook my head to clear it—I wasn't in pain and nothing seemed broken. I rose unsteadily to my feet. My left hand was cut from where I'd thrust it out to cushion my fall. The new explosion had occurred on the west side of Racine Street almost to the intersection with Carroll. I saw a fire truck burning, two police cars were in flames, and the fire among the buildings had been enhanced tenfold. Half a block farther north past Carroll Street on Racine, the lights of an all-night gas station burned brightly. I hated to think about the size of the explosion if the fire reached those storage tanks.

No one else stayed to dig in the debris and it was hopeless for me to keep digging on my own. People ran toward the victims who'd been nearest the new detonation. I was torn between hunting for Tom by myself or helping the newly injured. Frenzied chaos had returned. After several agonizing seconds, I joined the others.

Twenty feet from the burning fire truck, I saw a young cop on his knees. With an agonized moan, he put out a hand to keep himself from crumpling the rest of the way to the ground. I rushed forward. When I got to him, I saw that the skin on the left side of his face had been completely burned off. From his eye to his ear to below his chin, his cheek was a mealy mass of black bits and flecks of blood.

"Help me!" he gasped.

I didn't see a paramedic nearby who wasn't already overwhelmed with work. I helped the man walk to an ambulance. I sat him on the floor. He raised a hand toward his face.

I said, "I think maybe you shouldn't touch that."

He lowered his hand and took several deep breaths. "Thanks," he muttered. "There are some people worse off than me, you better go to them." Then he passed out. I made sure he was breathing, then pillowed his head as best I could with a blanket from the back of the ambulance.

For fifteen minutes, I carried stretchers filled with the wounded. I saw Kearn and his television crew giving assistance to those who were hurt. Their faces were scratched and bleeding. Good. Once I tripped over a smashed Minicam.

While I was helping tote a baby-faced fireman, someone ran by screaming, "There's more bombs! Everybody get out! Run for your lives!"

A few of the workers gave in to mad, blind panic and ran. Most of us moved on to the next point where we could help.

I hope never again to see the kind of agony and pain I saw that night. With each wounded victim, I saw another vision of what either explosion might have done to Tom. Only the immediacy of their pain kept me from obsessing about my lover. I don't know how many people I helped. I don't know why I didn't get sick at the torn and dismembered bodies. Probably because I didn't have time to think. Mostly I did as fire-department and paramedic people told me to.

I had long since begun to sweat. I realized moments later it wasn't just from the exertion. The second explosion had halted the fire-fighting efforts. The flames had burst into a conflagration devouring debris between where it had almost died and where I thought my lover might be. The only thing keeping it from the clinic was the firebreak made by the bulldozer, which was now on its side in the middle of the street. Much of the fire equipment was concentrated between the fire and the gas station. Only one stream of water was being poured on the fire between the clinic and the blaze. I saw another hose being set up.

In fairly short order, the newly injured were under the care of trained medical people or waiting transport to a hospital. A fire captain wearing a black fireman's coat with a horizontal yellow stripe was reorganizing about fifty of us to go back to hunting through the debris. He spoke through a bullhorn. "The order to evacuate hasn't come yet. There is a good chance there are more bombs at the site. You may lift a board and blow yourself and a lot of people into oblivion. You may lift a board and save some lives. Until the fire gets here, or we're told to move back, I'm going to keep trying. I won't order anyone to stay. If you're with us"—he almost grinned—"be as careful as possible."

After we'd been working a minute or two, I saw canine units arrive. In moments, handlers had their dogs stumbling through the busted fragments of the part of the city block that wasn't burning.

"Lot of dogs," somebody murmured near me.

A guy in a blue Chicago cop uniform looked in their direction. "I think a couple are bomb-sniffing dogs. The others are probably for finding survivors."

The man next to me said, "They're never going to be able

17

to stop the fire. This whole block is going to go. If there is anybody alive under all this, they're going to die."

I worked harder and faster. Sweat stung my eyes. I didn't take the time to wipe it away.

It might have been minutes later when the order passed. A cop in a starched white shirt with lieutenant insignia on it tapped me on the shoulder: "We're going to have to move back in a few minutes." They'd checked the fire in the direction of the gas station. The fire near us was still advancing.

Shouts rang out from two sections of the masses of destruction about ten feet apart. I rushed toward the one nearest me. One of the dogs was wagging its tail and letting out small yips. I hoped it was a "people" dog, not a "bomb" dog, and others were hastening toward it, and no one yelled to get back. When I was within several feet, I heard what sounded like the sobs of a small child. I remember trying to move debris while straining to catch another sound. Care could hardly be taken with the fire moving so close. While we could easily dislodge something and half a ton of debris could come crashing down on the trapped child, we had little choice.

Two minutes later a halt was called to the frantic digging. I could no longer hear the child. A slender man stripped off his outer gear, and with a rope tied at his waist, a miner's helmet on his head, he crawled headfirst into a narrow, dark opening. I joined the men clutching the rope linking us to the descending rescue worker. His head and shoulders disappeared. The rope went slack for a moment. As his waist and hips sank out of view, the rope became taut. The men beside me breathed heavily. Just as the descending man's knees were lost to view, the sounds of the child's crying began again.

18

A paramedic lying next to the man's legs yelled through a bullhorn, "Pull slowly." The ten of us grabbed the rope and slowly heaved backward.

Seconds later, man and child emerged. The kid was maybe three or four. He wore a bright yellow and red outfit. People cheered and clapped the rescuer on the back. A fireman hurried away with the child. Someone began untying the rope from around the rescuer's waist. He stopped the movement and shook his head. I was close enough to hear him mumble, "There's a body next to where I found the kid. Could be the mother, or maybe a day-care provider or a random victim. She's dead."

"You sure?"

"Yep."

Any elation I felt dissipated. I saw shoulders slump among the others nearby who had also heard.

The fire had leaped the alley in several places. The people around me began debating whether to stay and try to get the mother's body or leave and chance that it would burn. I looked to where the other group had been working.

Silhouetted against the encroaching flames were four men carrying a stretcher to a waiting ambulance. I caught a glimpse of the face. I thought it might be Tom. While rushing over, I tripped on the corner of an outthrust gray, metal filing cabinet. I twisted an ankle. The other leg sank into the fragments up to my knee. Several hands quickly jerked me back up.

"You okay?" a fireman asked.

"Yeah." I hobbled to the ambulance. I got there as the stretcher settled into the interior.

It was Tom.

At first I couldn't tell if he was breathing. His clothes were torn and shredded. He was covered in blood, dust, and soot. Paramedics began hooking him up to things. He can't be dead if they're working on him, I thought. I hoped.

"Is he alive?" I asked.

Someone grunted, "Yeah."

"Is he going to be okay?" I asked.

A paramedic stopped his swift, sure movements for several seconds and put his hand on my arm. "You must let us work. We're doing everything possible."

Each second of waiting was agony. For maybe a minute and a half they performed emergency functions. I couldn't tell if they were giving him minor medical attention and taking simple precautions or trying to stop him from dying. Gloria Dellios hurried up. "Is he all right?"

"He's unconscious. They're working on him."

There was a much smaller explosion. I looked. It was a van from one of the television stations. No one had moved it from the path of the approaching fire. Its gas tank had exploded. A crowd of rescue workers and several camera crews from other television stations rushed past us toward the new calamity. Those of us gathered around this ambulance were jostled for several moments.

Then a low voice close to my ear said, "You're next, faggot."

I whirled around. A throng of passersby were frantically rushing through the confusion, and any one of them could have said that. Even if I caught up to the group of people the voice had come from, I could never pick out which person had said it.

I heard one of the paramedics say into a phone, "We'll be arriving at your location in four minutes." The ambulance engine started. They began to close the rear doors. I forgot thoughts of chasing whoever it was. I knew I wanted to stay with Tom.

"I'm his lover," I said. "I'm going with you."

No one objected or stood in my way. I hopped in. I scrunched down next to the stretcher. I held Tom's hand and watched him breathe. The paramedic monitored devices. No one spoke for the short trip to St. Michael's Hospital, just north of Division Street on Racine. I knew they'd be rushing him away as soon as we pulled up.

As we slowed to a stop, I said, "I love you, Tom." I knew he couldn't hear me, but I needed to say it.

Ambulances jammed the entrance to the trauma center. We parked in the middle of the street. They hurried Tom into the hospital. Inside the emergency room, paramedics, doctors, nurses, and hospital staff were in a frenzy of activity.

Before I settled down to a bout of worrying that would make Tom proud, I called his mom and dad. His mom's a brick, but I knew the news shook her. It would anybody. They would drive in from the far suburbs as quickly as possible.

Half an hour later Gloria Dellios joined me on the blue plastic chairs in the waiting room.

"No word," I said.

She shook her head. "It's ghastly. The count is up to twenty confirmed dead. Two of them were in the clinic. They weren't able to find everyone before the fire got to the building. I'm afraid the toll will go much higher."

I tried to think of something comforting to say. I like to think of myself as innately courteous. I may not always say the right thing, but at least I don't usually say something stupid. I couldn't think of a thing.

Over an hour later Brandon Kearn walked up without a camera crew in tow. The entire back of his blazer was in shreds. A bandage covered his right hand. He had stitches on his right ear and in the middle of a newly shaved spot on the back of his head. The rest of his hair, which often looked cemented in place, was wildly askew and covered in dust and dotted with blood. He sat down next to me.

"You okay?" he asked.

"I've got a few superficial cuts that some kind of tech person stitched up. My ears stopped ringing only a little while ago. Between emergencies a doctor glanced at me. He said I'm fine. I feel okay."

"You waiting here for someone?"

"Is this an interview?"

"I'm a little too tired and a little too personally involved to get into a professional mode right now. My boss told me to get medical attention and go home. He sounded pissed. I guess I was supposed to keep the cameras rolling instead of trying to help. I gave one live interview while I was bleeding. I think I hate reporters. Not a good attitude, I'm afraid, for somebody who's in the profession. I'm done for the night and might get fired."

"For helping people? No boss is that nuts. You'll be on all the talk shows as the reporter hero."

"Being a hero isn't quite what I expected it to be. Messier, dirtier, uglier, and meaner. Setting off another bomb to explode when the rescue workers are present is insanely cruel."

"The whole thing is total madness," Dellios said. "Too much hate. That's what's wrong with society."

Kearn nodded at her. "Who are you?"

"Gloria Dellios, the head administrator at the Human Services Clinic."

"I should probably try and interview you for background," Kearn said.

"Not now."

"No, later. Hell of a thing to happen."

Dellios said, "Unfortunately, anyone who works in a women's clinic has to be ready for this kind of thing, although nobody's been through something this massive. No matter how many tragedies anybody has been through, I don't think they'd be prepared for this. I'm sure I'll be here all night until I know how all my people are."

"I appreciate that," I said.

"I'm one of the lucky ones. It isn't a burden." Dellios touched my arm. "The few times I met Tom, he was always humorous and friendly. He made jokes about working in the basement, hidden away from the clients."

I said, "Maybe that's what saved his life."

Kearn said, "I know about your lover from the news coverage of you coming out. Why was he working at the clinic?"

"Is that really important for you to know right this instant?"

Kearn seemed to revive a little. "I've always been curious about why you decided to—"

I cut him off. "No interview."

"Sorry," Kearn said.

"How come you were on WBBM?" I asked. "I thought you worked for MCT."

"I do. I was the first reporter on the scene. The feed went to any local station that wanted to pick it up. For a while CNN was using it."

"How'd you know I was there?" I asked.

"One of the camera guys noticed you. Why?"

"I was wondering how you picked me out of so many in the chaos."

"You're one of the most recognizable faces in Chicago. If you turned out to be a hero or a great camera shot, you'd be a big story. Picture Michael Jordan rescuing a baby from a burning building. It'd make the front page of every paper on the planet. It wasn't odd that you were singled out."

"I guess not."

Kearn patted my shoulder and said, "I hope your lover makes it." After I thanked him, he got up and left.

I had no concept of how much time I needed to let pass before requesting or demanding information. Brief lulls in the emergency room were followed by bouts of frantic action. When it finally seemed that the lulls were more prevalent, I hunted for the right person to talk to. When I finally found the doctor who had treated Tom, I asked the most basic question: "Is he going to live?"

The doctor said, "He has no life-threatening injuries that we are aware of at this time. We'll know more after we can do more tests."

Back in the waiting room, I stood in a corner. Dellios was off talking to other relatives of victims. All of the chairs in the waiting room were filled. People stood in clumps all the way up and down the halls. Most waited in muffled silence. One youngster about ten kept asking, "Is Daddy going to die?" Mercifully, he finally fell asleep, but not soon enough.

I shut my eyes. For the first time, the images I'd seen flooded my memory. The one of a cop screaming in agony and clutching at the place where his left leg used to be came back more clearly than I ever want a memory to come back. I hurried to the washroom and puked. When I finished barfing my guts out, I washed my face. When my stomach was under control, I returned to the waiting room.

. . .

The next thing I remember is Tom's parents, siblings, nephews, and nieces beginning to gather. The traffic coming into the Loop had been totally snarled. With so much emergency equipment, the number of streets blocked off, and the gawkers trying to get to the tragedy, it took them nearly two hours to make the normally fifty-minute drive.

I love his family. His mom and dad treat us the same as his straight brothers and sister and their in-laws, but at the moment, I didn't want to talk much to anyone. When big emotions come, lots of times I close down. Some of that comes from my upbringing, some from my profession. Shutting out all distractions is an important skill for a major league pitcher. Early in my relationship with Tom, my retreating inside myself caused some problems. If we had a fight, instead of discussing things, I'd shut myself in. That hurt both of us. Now, although sometimes it takes me a while, I can be open and vulnerable with him. But I often still have the problem with others.

I gave his family what little information I had, that he was being monitored closely and was not in immediate danger of dying.

I was annoyed at the presence of so many people, particularly the ones under ten. I enjoy Tom's nephews and nieces, especially the younger ones. I probably have a better time with them than he does. He might be a teacher, but he only deals with high school kids. Throw him in a barrel of kids below the age of ten, and he's pretty lost. The younger they are, the worse Tom handles them. Right now, however, I wanted them all to be silent and go away. Hushed waiting made more sense to me, and I'd rather have been alone. At one point his four-year-old nephew, Josh, tugged on my hand and asked to be picked up and held. He rested his head against my shoulder and said, "Don't be sad, Uncle Scott.

Uncle Tom is going to be okay. He promised to take me to the zoo next week. He always keeps his promises."

I held him close. I wanted the comfort and simplicity of beliefs and promises in a child's world. In minutes he fell asleep. I wished I could find comfort and sleep so easily.

◣ 4 ◢

By three in the morning all those under eighteen years of age had been packed off for home. Tom's mom and dad, older brother, and I kept vigil.

When I looked up about quarter after four, I saw Ken McCutcheon, the owner of the security firm I had hired for protection when I made pubic appearances. He had a cup of coffee in his hand. He stood unobtrusively in the hallway leading to the waiting room. He saw my look and nodded at me.

I strolled over. McCutcheon looked like a college wrestler in the 160-pound class. Golden blond hair, muscles perfectly sculpted, eyes intensely blue, stance always casual. He was dressed simply—a long-sleeve, white dress shirt, a dark blue tie, faded blue jeans, no belt, white socks, and running shoes. Today he also wore an unzipped black leather jacket. He spoke in a soft tenor voice. He rarely smiled.

McCutcheon was always armed, but never obviously so. When I was hunting for a guard, several friends had highly recommended him and his firm. Frankly, I thought he was too pretty and too young to be effective, but he had proved his worth to me when he'd handled a potential raving loony.

This one guy had showed up at three straight appearances. He always sat as close to the podium as possible. He kept his shirtsleeves rolled up so anyone who glanced at him could see the swastika tattooed on his massive right biceps. He would stare fixedly at me throughout the event. I swear I never saw him blink. He had horror-movie eyes—you could see the white entirely around the washed-out-blue iris. I would have found it almost clownish if I hadn't been so spooked. He never asked questions or talked to anyone else. The first time I noticed him, he gave me the creeps. The second time he showed up, I also saw him afterward in the parking lot. He was walking toward my car. That's when I hired McCutcheon. When the guy showed up for the third time, McCutcheon cornered him in the parking lot next to my car. I was too far away to hear what was said, but after that, whoever he was, he stayed away.

I once asked McCutcheon what he had said to the guy. "I reasoned with him" was all he ever told me. If people began to crowd around me after a talk, McCutcheon placed himself between them and me. He didn't threaten or push or shove. People just seemed to give him space. He had a sense of presence that always seemed to work.

When he drove me places, he seldom spoke, rarely engaged in idle conversation, and never used more words than necessary. I'd hired him for his presence, not his personality, so his not talking much didn't bother me. Tom sometimes said McCutcheon gave him the creeps. McCutcheon was quiet, unobtrusive, and efficient. The others in his firm, mostly guys his age or slightly older, had either copied his demeanor or were similarly trained. I felt safe with them around.

The friends who'd recommended him to me told exotic stories about McCutcheon, each stranger than the last. They speculated wildly about an erratic and erotic life with James Bond–type adventures including male and female lovers around the globe. The rumors included murky tales of connections to the CIA; that he'd done time in a Turkish prison; that he'd been part of assassination plots against a variety of foreign leaders; that he'd been part of any number of well-known terrorist organizations; that he was the leader of a gay death squad; that he was a straight hit man for various wealthy gay clients. I hired him because two people I trusted implicitly swore by him and his firm's expertise and willingness to sacrifice themselves at moments of danger. When I asked for a résumé, he said, "Either you trust the people who recommended me or you don't. If you don't trust them, I'd rather you didn't hire me."

Another time I asked if he wasn't kind of young to have his own agency. All he'd said in return was "How old should I be?" After that I stopped asking questions.

That morning I stood next to him in the hall. He said, "One of my employees saw your picture on the late news. He called me. Thought I should check out what happened."

"How'd you know Tom was hurt?"

"I didn't. I knew that you were out in public and that nobody from my firm was with you. I got the answering service to put a call directly through, but there was no answer. I know Tom works at that clinic. We've picked him up there once or twice after an event of yours. I figured I better stop by—you had been recognized at the scene and lots of people knew you were there. I couldn't find you and I didn't know where you were, so I tried calling the hospitals until I got to this one."

"I was threatened." I told him what had happened.

"I'll stay close. Bombers often come back to help at the scene to see their handiwork and revel in the chaos. If I can find you, so can anyone."

I introduced him to the family. They showed little curiosity about his being there. They were aware of the security measures Tom and I had taken in the past few years.

Around five they told us that Tom had been moved to the intensive care unit on the third floor. We moved our vigil up there.

By six in the morning there had been no change in Tom's condition. The doctor told me that the good news was no bones were broken. The bad news was that they couldn't tell the extent of his internal injuries. They were most worried about head trauma. The doctor had ordered more tests. Tom might wake up, or he might not, but we would not do ourselves any good staying awake and hanging around the hospital.

Tom's parents and I agreed on rotating assignments for the vigil. I'd been awake and there the longest and I was exhausted. They would stay and call with any news.

McCutcheon and I rode the elevator down to the first floor. The doors opened onto the hospital foyer. Television cameras and reporters were strewn about the room. A spokesman for the hospital was making a statement and seemed to be trying to organize the chaos the reporters were helping to accentuate. I was spotted. A wave of media people rushed toward me. A young couple, the woman significantly pregnant and being wheeled forward, were between us and the reporters. The woman's angry squawks as they massed behind her gurney gave them pause. Television lights focused on me. McCutcheon led me slowly to the right. They fired questions. I halted. I was used to the media's need for something. I'd been brusque with Kearn at the scene and had refused all interviews in the emergency room, but I could give them something.

The man and pregnant woman gazed at the chaos around them. "Aren't you Scott Carpenter the baseball player?" the husband asked.

I nodded and smiled. "Let's make way for them, shall we?"

The herd of media parted to form a path for the pregnant couple. When they were free, I focused on a reporter I recognized and nodded to her. She asked, "We heard your lover was in the explosion. How is he?"

I said, "The doctors are doing all they can."

Someone shouted, "Is he getting special treatment because you're famous?"

"Everyone who knows someone caught in this catastrophe is concerned. I'm not special. I waited like everyone else. Tom is alive. My heart goes out to those who've lost a loved one."

I turned quickly. McCutcheon caught the movement. We forged a path through the mingling horde and out a side door. McCutcheon drove me back to my car under the el tracks near the scene. He drove a grayish black Hummer. I don't get the attraction of those vehicles. Yeah, I know they're supposed to be butcher than all get out, but they're noisy, clunky, difficult to maneuver, and they can cost up to a hundred thousand dollars. I glanced around the seat and tried to figure out what it was that made it cost so much. A cursory inspection showed me nothing.

As usual McCutcheon said little as he drove.

We couldn't get near the scene of the explosion. The entire area was cordoned off. We could see the muted chaos from several blocks away. I saw three fire hoses still pouring water on the remnants of the city block, although at the moment only whiffs of smoke oozed from a few spots. Police and fire department personnel hunted through parts of the wreckage that were sufficiently cooled. I doubted if there was much hope for any more survivors. The second blast and unchecked fire had eliminated any possibility of that.

Ken drove past my car slowly. It was barely first light. Trails of mist floated over the scene. The square arches of the el tracks over the pavement created a twilight world during the brightest day. At the moment, each strut struck me more as menace than support. McCutcheon trained his spotlight on any dark corners. When he decided all was safe, he stopped opposite my car.

"We should get Tom's truck out of here too," I said.

"I can follow you home, then bring you back."

I began to open my door. It was early enough that traffic was still light. I had to wait for a van to pass, then together we slowly crossed the street toward my vehicle. McCutcheon didn't look at me. Just like the Secret Service seldom looks at the president. They are on the alert for dangers as was McCutcheon now.

I was tired, worried about Tom, and in need of sleep. I doubted if all McCutcheon's precautions were necessary. I couldn't imagine someone who'd seen me at the fire being able to figure out which of these cars was mine.

Above, an el car thundered forward from the Loop. I paused. I didn't want to be under the tracks when its jangling rumble passed overhead. At the best of times the el train noise was a major annoyance. Another train hurtled toward us from the west. McCutcheon and I stopped. The cacophony was terrible. Then the ground shook. Tom's truck blew up.

.5.

For the second time in a few hours, I was knocked to the ground. It was more instinct than conscious decision that I got my hands out in front of me and broke my fall. McCutcheon and I scrambled away from the intense heat. Down the block about fifty feet, we stopped. I sat myself on the curb on the far side of the street from the burning wreck. At this distance I could barely feel the heat from the flames. Bits of pavement were gouged into my already begrimed palms. I picked out the larger bits, then dusted my hands on my jeans to dislodge the remaining dirt. McCutcheon stood over me. As we watched Tom's truck burn, random thoughts and fears flitted through my mind. They centered on who would do this, and how did they know his truck was here?

I was determined to do all I could to make the terror I was feeling disappear. I was angry at the perpetrators and frightened for Tom's life and my own. Mixed with fear and anger were feelings of dread and hopelessness. I already knew that there was no way to stop the unreasonably angry and the totally mad from wreaking destruction on the rest of us. I guess we all know this, but how often do we really face it? I'm not sure if I was trying to keep myself from thinking about the accumulated terror of the night or from looking for real answers. I realized I'd never come this close to dying before. That scared the hell out of me. I pictured myself getting into Tom's truck and being instantly immolated. I threw up what little was left in my stomach.

People from the scene of the clinic explosion rushed toward the flames of this new terror. A fire engine arrived in less than five minutes. Tom's truck was a complete loss, but they worked to keep the flames from spreading to the other cars or melting the struts of the superstructure on which the el ran.

A mess of cops showed up. I told the first ones I was the lover of the owner of the truck and that he'd been hurt in the earlier bombing. A crowd of onlookers and a few camera crews trickled over. I was recognized early on, but McCutcheon and I got to stand inside the crime-scene tape and be less hassled.

A uniformed cop took down basic information. Then Larry Jantoro, a Chicago police detective, showed up. He and McCutcheon nodded to each other—wasn't hard to figure they knew one another—and Jantoro addressed his first questions to McCutcheon.

Full dawn broke as McCutcheon gave him the details about what had happened from the moment we turned onto this street. When Jantoro asked me about my movements that night, I told him everything. As I explained, he took notes and asked questions. The one he repeated most often was, "Did you come back here at all after you arrived?"

I hadn't. After I finished, Jantoro said, "We've got to figure out if someone knew this was actually your buddy's truck, or if you and him were a victim of random chance. This auxiliary parking lot for the clinic may have been a secondary target or the killer's last cruel joke to hurt people who thought they were safe."

"Or it could have been a planned attack on us," I said.

"Anything's possible," Jantoro said in that grudging tone that meant he didn't really think it was probable. "You've got guards. You might think about hiring a few more."

The police had sent for the bomb squad to inspect all the other cars in the vicinity. I was unwilling to wait the extra time. I could get my car later.

"The world has lost its mind," I said as Jantoro walked away.

McCutcheon nodded. "Looks that way a lot. I'd be out of a job if it wasn't."

"Is that security-guard humor?" I asked.

"Just an observation."

"Somebody could be watching me right now." I glanced around at the still-darkened buildings and the shadows under the el that might not dissipate even in the brightest light of day. "This is more immediate than all the threats during the season. What am I supposed to do now?"

"You could obsess about it, but what's the point? You're already alert and wary." McCutcheon and I talked as we got into his Hummer and headed toward Lake Shore Drive. "Think about it this way. Most likely they were after the abortion clinic. It's unlikely that it's about you or Tom."

"But not impossible."

"No, not impossible." McCutcheon wasn't as dismissive as Jantoro, but he was in the same ballpark.

"Remember, I was specifically threatened, Tom's truck

was blown up, and my lover is in the hospital. That's one hell of a lot of coincidences. Sounds like more than random chance to me."

"You really think they blew up an entire city block to make you miserable?"

"Well, if you put it that way, no, except—"

"Specifically personal terrorism isn't the general rule. Bomb the clinic. Add a couple of secondary explosions. For a terrorist that's all in a day's work. People in the crowd recognize you, which happens often. Someone who recognizes you doesn't like you. They make a threat. Most likely an idle threat. If it scared you—"

"It did."

"—then he accomplished his purpose. The more you sit and brood the worse it gets."

"But specific terrorism does happen. Look at those doctors who worked at clinics. They got murdered."

"But this wasn't an individual assassination. If someone really wanted to kill you, they'd probably succeed."

"Then why did I hire you?"

"Same reason everybody does. If there was a concerted frontal attack on you, we'd try to stop it. Those rarely happen. Mostly we're a deterrent. The attackers or killers have to take us into account. What we're really here for is to make the client feel more secure. You knew that when you hired me."

He didn't have to say, "I told you so." I remembered the earlier conversation when he'd explained the limits on what his firm could do.

As we turned onto Michigan Avenue, I thought I'd try again. "What does it mean that they knew which car was his?"

"You want a vast conspiracy or random chance?"

"Neither. I want to go to sleep."

"Random chance happens more often than we care to admit. That's why it's called random chance."

"Is that supposed to be comforting? I think the bomb was meant for Tom and me, and I'm frightened. Can I walk outside of my home? Going with me to events is one thing. Having you around my every waking minute does not sound like the way I want to live. Do Tom and I need to keep you around forever?"

"What did you think was going to happen after you became the most public gay figure in America?"

"How could anyone have planned for that?" I sighed. "I expected to be a focal point, not a target."

"It's not an easy reality to face. The more careful and more sensible take as many precautions as they can."

"I'm not sure if I'm careful or sensible at this point. Sometimes I think everybody is threatening me. This doesn't make sense."

"What's happened so far makes sense to someone who is probably certifiably insane. How you live your life in the face of that insanity is your choice. You can sit in your apartment and wait for the world to come to you, or you can make decisions and do something about it. You've been under threat since you announced you were going to pitch after coming out."

6

I will never forget pitching in that first game. The terror and joy of those moments is seared in my memory. The announcement of my impending mound appearance caused an immense sensation. I was to be the first athlete who was openly gay while still active in a major sport. Within fifteen minutes of the announcement that I would pitch, all the tickets for the game were sold out, and more press credentials were requested than for a World Series game. Tickets were being scalped at over a thousand dollars apiece. Security was unprecedented—everyone attending the game had to walk through metal detectors and all bags were searched. The cops told me I set a record for number of death threats in a twenty-four-hour period.

Hundreds of other calls came from people threatening to cancel their season tickets. Some threatened not to go to another baseball game as long as I was in the league. A slew of supportive calls came too, but none of these were what I was afraid of.

Several prominent sports people have said that it would be easier for a convicted felon, returning from a stint in prison, to play on a professional sport team than it would be for an openly gay person. There's no question there are gay people in major sports. A few who compete in individual sports have come out—Louganis, Navratilova, Galindo—but these are the exceptions, not the rule.

I was unprepared for what greeted me when I went out to begin warming up that day. As I walked out of the clubhouse, I heard an uncharacteristically loud murmuring from the stands. I could see blue-uniformed cops blocking the light in the doorway to the field.

My favorite catcher, Morty Hamilton, was behind me. Morty wasn't that great with a bat, but he threw himself with reckless abandon at anything pitched to him. He set the record for fewest passed balls in a season. He said, "I ain't never been shot at."

"This isn't a day for dying," I remember saying.

Five feet from the dugout I stopped and took a deep breath. I walked into the sunshine and stopped again. Thirty thousand people were already in the stands. As I jogged onto the field, they rose to their feet cheering and applauding. I turned around 360 degrees. It was hours before game time and the stands were nearly filled.

"Don't sound like a lynching," Morty said.

I nodded.

After a few moments, he nudged me. "We gonna get started or you gonna stare at them?"

The crowd clustered as close as they were allowed to the playing field during batting practice. Police officers stood at every egress to the field and at the end of the aisles next to the field. After I finished stretching and doing wind sprints, I began to warm up. There were calls of encouragement and scattered applause at every pitch.

It was the largest crowd in the history of the park. When I walked out to pitch in the first inning, the ovation continued for five minutes. A few in the reserved boxes were sitting down. As far as I could see, the rest were on their feet. Thousands were waving little rainbow flags. I saw numerous rainbow banners unfurled. I could see groups of leathermen, clots of drag queens, and thousands of regularly dressed men and women.

After the national anthem, they didn't sit down. They roared and cheered for each strike I threw. They booed at each ball. Each out caused a wave of thunderous cheering. After the third out that inning the noise swelled to a crescendo. As I strolled to the dugout, I gave the crowd a slight tip of my cap. They went nuts.

Most of them sat down as my team came to bat. When the first batter stepped in, the singing started. First it was "We Shall Overcome," then "Somewhere over the Rainbow," then various show tunes. It was a gay crowd after all.

I pitched a one-hitter. Morty said I never threw harder. While I was on the field, I don't remember the cheering ever stopping. Even when the game ended, they kept on. Hundreds of cops stood on the field as I made a circuit of the stadium. Even then they didn't stop. I came out of the clubhouse three times before they finally began streaming out of the stadium.

In every city it had been the same. Threats. Tickets sold out in minutes, record crowds, wild cheering, rainbow flags, singing. In one city someone had shouted out, "Sinner." The cheering didn't stop for fifteen minutes after that. The shouter was escorted out, probably more for his safety. I won twenty-eight games that year. We didn't come close to getting into the play-offs, but Chicago is used to losing baseball teams.

I said to McCutcheon, "I thought I was past all that. The season's over."

"It's never going to be over as long as you're alive."

I knew that already. I just wasn't sure I wanted to be reminded of it at that moment. Because you aren't the one to say something first or you forget the truth in a moment of high emotion doesn't mean you haven't thought of it or don't realize it.

As he pulled into the circle drive of my building, I said, "I don't know what the hell I'm supposed to do with the rest of my life."

"Wallowing in self-pity is probably not a good option. I'd stick with round-the-clock security at least until this is cleared up. It's more likely to be helpful than pity."

"I'm not sure I need a lecture on my response to this whole situation. You're a guard, not my keeper."

"What do you want me to say?"

I didn't want to sit and brood. I wanted to hurt someone. Which is how all this mess probably started. Someone wanting to lash out and hurt. Tom would say it's more complicated than that. He's always looking for deep psychological motivations and hidden meanings.

Finally I said, "I want you to tell me that you have a magic formula to make this all go away."

"Maybe you should try that self-pity thing for a little longer."

I managed a brief smile. "How would the twenty-four-hour-a-day security work?"

"It's pricey."

"Cost is not the problem." Before this, security had been easily planned. We'd go over my schedule of public appearances, and people from his firm would be assigned. The number of guards would depend on the venue and how large a crowd was expected.

He explained, "For today, call whenever you're ready to go out, I'll respond immediately. I can have someone ready in half an hour, probably less. If you know the night before, it is easier to assign somebody, but we're just starting and this is a special case. You have the firm's number, my private office number, my home number, and my pager number. No matter what time, just call me."

"I could get used to hating living like this." I shook my head. "I'm going to get some sleep." I got out of the car.

Just before I entered the private elevator to the penthouse, I looked back at the entrance. McCutcheon was watching me from his Hummer, waiting until I was safely inside.

7

Each time, just before I felt myself finally drifting off to sleep, I'd get flashes of the terror I had witnessed hours before. I don't remember falling asleep. I woke after maybe three hours in the middle of a nightmare of torn and bleeding people reaching out charred hands for help. The nightmare images still swirling in my mind boded ill for the healing power of sleep. The waking memory of the reality I had seen was equally as frightening.

I tossed and turned for another hour, vainly trying to nod off again. In addition to the restlessness from the chaos and the fear of the last few hours, I missed Tom's sleeping next to me. I know I'm on the road half the spring and summer without him, but even then I miss him. When he's supposed to be there and he's not, I don't feel right.

I called the hospital. There was no change in Tom's condition. I turned on the noon news on MCT. They had extensive coverage of the bombing. The number of dead was up to thirty-four: fourteen in the clinic, five in the deli, four in a residential hotel, four in a twenty-four-hour print shop, three in the health club, three passersby, and one person working late in his upscale office on a Saturday night. Hundreds more were injured. They showed extensive pictures of the children injured in the ice cream shop next to the Fattatuchis' deli. I felt especially sorry for the parents clutching frightened kids, the bright lights and cameras intruding on their suffering. I wished I could comfort the little ones in some way.

Since so many people had died in the other venues, it was not officially decided that the clinic had been the target of the bombing. No group had called to take credit for the explosions. The reporter made much of the fact that last night there had been a banquet in Chicago honoring anti-abortion protesters. Most of the prominent names in the movement had been in town, and all were being questioned.

My name was mentioned as one of the rescue workers, and as part of the speculation about why this had been done. Also discussed was Tom's truck being blown up and what possible connection that could have to the earlier bombings. The reporter on the scene claimed that the device in Tom's truck had been a limpet mine. I had no idea what that meant.

I saw Brandon Kearn being interviewed. Someone had gotten him a new blazer, his hair was cemented back in place, and he'd had a chance to clean up. Numerous close-ups showed his stitches prominently.

The last person interviewed was Lyle Gibson. He was the leader of the protesters from outside the clinic. He said, "My organization abhors violence, but those who murder children can hardly expect to avoid the consequences . . ." I turned it off. I didn't want to listen to disclaimers designed to keep people from getting arrested for incitement to murder rather than being true expressions of sorrow and regret.

My press agent called. He burbled with excitement:

"Think about it. What more positive image for gay people than that of you heroically rescuing someone at one of the biggest disasters in urban history? You were there and helping. There's all kinds of pictures of you being shown on the all-news stations."

"I don't really care."

He blathered on, "I've got requests for interviews from half a dozen major news outlets so far. I'm sure there'll be more. You could really cash in on—"

I spoke over his excitement, "Later, if there is a fund-raiser to help the injured children, I'd be happy to be part of it. Right now my concern is my lover being unconscious in the hospital. I'll call you." And I hung up.

I called McCutcheon's private number at home. He didn't sound sleepy.

I said, "I'd like to try and get some answers from the police about what happened."

"Like what?"

"Like everything. What happened, why, who did it, and if it's connected to Tom and me."

"I can try and call a friend in the department, or we can try and talk to the cop from last night."

"I'd like to try both."

An hour later, after I'd eaten, McCutcheon brought over Clayton Pulver. Pulver was in his late twenties or early thirties. He wore his hair slightly over his ears, and he had a mustache. He wore scuffed cowboy boots, faded black jeans, and a red and pink thunder-and-lightning western shirt.

McCutcheon explained, "Clayton's in a tactical unit. He hears things."

The tactical units in Chicago are cops in casual dress.

They are involved in basic anticrime work, such as setting up narcotics stings. They are the ultimate street cops with the toughness, street smarts, pride, and bluster that come from dealing with the darkest side of police work.

Pulver sprawled his skinny frame onto one of the white couches. He placed his right ankle on his left knee. McCutcheon sat on the arm of the couch. I was in a chair near the floor-to-ceiling windows with the John Hancock building in the background.

Pulver said first, "I like the way you pitch. Took balls to walk out on the mound with all the pressure." His flat Midwestern tones contrasted with his down-on-the-ranch outfit.

"Thanks," I said simply.

He entwined his fingers and placed them behind his head. His eyes swept around the penthouse. "Hell of a place you got."

McCutcheon said, "Clayton, get on with it. What do you know about the bombing?"

Pulver grinned. His teeth were sparkling white. "I'll tell you what I can because I owe Kenny here a big favor. I don't like talking outside the department."

I nodded. "I appreciate whatever you can tell me." I'd never heard anyone call McCutcheon "Kenny." His employees always referred to him as Mr. McCutcheon.

Pulver rubbed his narrow fingers on his pants. "Have you heard the best rumor yet? This one's been on the Internet since a few minutes after the explosion."

McCutcheon said, "If it's on the Internet, it must be an absolute crock."

"Yeah, but you get the most fun out of the Internet in a tragedy like this. It's like the court jester in a Shakespearean tragedy."

"Pulver?" McCutcheon added exasperation to his tone.

48

"The Internet rumor is that the bombing had nothing to do with the clinic. That, in fact, across the alley from the clinic there was a secret terrorist cell called the Tools of Satan with headquarters in one of those residential hotels that was destroyed. At that point the theory gets muddled. One idea is that the terrorists accidentally blew themselves away. Another is that a rival group of terrorists decided to strike against them. Supposedly no one would suspect it was a simple act of murder. Everyone would think the attack was aimed at the clinic."

I asked, "Has anyone confirmed the existence of a terrorist hiding place?"

"Not a smidgen of fact to the rumor, so far. That's the best kind of thing to get on the Internet. Something faintly plausible and absolutely undeniable."

"I'm ready to discount it," McCutcheon said.

"Everybody pretty much does. That's the beauty of that kind of rumor. It could be true. And it's even better if it's denied by the police because someone will find some occupant of the area who has a third cousin living in the Middle East. Said cousin is probably a grocery clerk in Tunisia who has a brother-in-law who was in the Libyan army thirty years ago. That person will make half-baked claims that officials will scoff at." Pulver snapped his fingers. "Sounds like a conspiracy to me."

"Pulver," McCutcheon said, "can we just get on with it?"

"Okay. I called a few people. Here's the deal. The bomb in your friend's car is throwing the investigation off somewhat. Bomb the clinic, second bomb to kill rescue workers, that's happened in a number of these. Why a third bomb? Why your lover's truck? It was in the clinic's lot. Might have been a fluke, or of course, someone could have known it was his specifically. Terrorizing abortion clinics isn't big news, although killing that many people at a clinic is a record. One big problem is nobody knows how you fit in."

"I've gotten several zillion death threats."

"But not in connection with an abortion clinic. If somebody does bomb one of these places, it's most likely a political statement. I know everybody expects this to be a right-wing conspiracy. These organizations aren't shy about taking credit. Half the time that's the point. But we don't have that here. No one's called to claim responsibility." Pulver shook his head. "Kenny told me about the threat you got last night. No one knows how significant it is. It might have been a coincidence. A lot of people don't like you, and you're one of the most recognized people in the city."

"Ken and I have been through all that speculation."

Pulver resumed, "I heard it was a limpet mine that got your buddy's truck."

"That means nothing to me."

"It gets set off by vibrations. Normally it wouldn't have blown until someone got in the car and started the engine, but the two el trains passing at the same time caused just enough movement to set it off."

"I would have been killed."

"Yep. It wasn't set for blowing up the car on a timing device. Death was the goal, not just destruction. That's the bit that indicates it was more personal rather than political. I think it's highly unlikely the bomber or bombers used that kind of explosive device because it was the only one he could get."

"Maybe he got a deal," McCutcheon said. "Buy three rockets, two mortars, and you get this limpet mine thrown in for free."

Pulver said, "And maybe a lower interest rate on his payments, which he doesn't have to make until next year. Or a frequent-terrorist discount."

Their attempts at sarcasm were more humor than I was in the mood for.

"What else?" I asked.

"The bomber knew what he was doing and planned well." Pulver leaned forward and placed his elbows on his knees. He held my gaze for several moments, then said, "Lots of people are going to be asking you questions about this. Kenny's a friend and I'm in your corner. I think it would help if we went over you and your friend's movements the last few days."

"Am I under suspicion?"

"Nope."

"How could I know anything?"

"You probably don't, but if someone is specifically after you, then maybe you'll give me a hint that will begin helping us get to the bottom of this."

"But I couldn't possibly be involved."

"Somebody had a lot of other cars to choose from last night. Your buddy's truck got bombed. If it means anything beyond random chance, we've got to ask."

It seemed pointless to me, but I went ahead and gave him a detailed account of my movements the day before.

When I finished, Pulver shook his head. "Somebody'd have to be watching you both awful close and be awful lucky to be able to plant that bomb on such short notice in Mason's truck. That's presuming all three bombings had something to do with you."

"Could they have?"

"Anything's possible." At least Pulver didn't sound as dismissive as Jantoro had the night before.

"Who'd be willing to go to such great lengths to hurt me and Tom?"

"Do you read your own press coverage?" Pulver asked.

"Okay, stupid question. Sorry."

Pulver continued, "But why wait until last night to go to those lengths? And why kill all those other people? Venting anger at you by hurting your lover makes some sense, not killing all those other people as well." Pulver shook his head. "I don't think it was *all* about you. I'm just not sure it wasn't somehow about you. Putting the bomb in Mason's truck specifically makes things complicated and awkward. Your killer has to realize he was there, find the truck, get the bomb—"

I interrupted, "Unless they followed him from home."

"How would they know he was going out? If they knew where you lived, why did they wait until this time when he went out? It's too much coincidence. We need a lot more information before being able to say anything for sure."

"Do the police have any clues at all?"

"Tons of them literally. The main explosion was a truck bomb, big goddamn thing. They're trying to assemble parts of the vehicle that they think contained the bomb to try and determine the manufacturer and ownership. That stuff could also tell them about the nature of the blast, and they might find traces of chemical residue for analysis. They'll probably be examining what's left of that block for weeks. Every piece of debris will be carefully sifted. They're talking to the survivors. They've got hundreds of possible witnesses, and they're trying to pin down the movements of anybody who was around that block."

"What about all those prominent protesters being in town?"

"Cops don't like coincidences. All those people have the

52

alibi of having been at the dinner, but one of them could have parked the truck and strolled over."

I said, "Someone must have seen a truck with that much explosive."

"If they've found out something from witnesses, I haven't heard about it. With that much destruction, I was told the bomber would need at least a thousand pounds of explosives. They're also going through the background of every person who had a business on that block, of every employee of all the shops, all the residents, and of course, of every person who was killed. So far nothing has come up."

"They had Timothy McVeigh within a few hours," I said. "They had a reason to question that Eric Robert Rudolph, in those bombings in the South, in less than a day. It didn't take them long to identify the suspects who shot those doctors at the abortion clinics."

"I read the same things you do. My sources say they aren't even close to a suspect. I know they've hauled in most of the regular protesters who show up outside the clinic. They've got nothing out of them so far. They had to let them go. Some of them have been out there every day for years. Lots of these folks are dedicated to their cause. That doesn't make them nuts. Setting off a bomb does. The police keep current files on the repeat protesters. I don't know whether or not any of them have a background of violence."

"You don't need a background," I said, "just a computer connected to the Internet."

"Expertise in bomb making is no longer necessary," Pulver agreed, "but there's also a psychological profile."

"And what if you've got a smart bomber who doesn't fit the profile?" I asked.

"An angry, violent person who has never given a hint of

being sociopathic destroys a city block and doesn't care how many he killed, and nobody's noticed they're slightly off-kilter? I don't think so."

"Lots of people holing up in cabins in Montana these days," I said. "They keep to themselves and avoid their neighbors. Nuttiness is rampant, and I bet it isn't that hard to hide."

"I've got a hunting cabin in Montana," Pulver said.

"Is telling me that supposed to comfort me?"

"I guess you can take it for what it's worth." Pulver didn't sound angry or annoyed.

McCutcheon asked, "Didn't I read in the *New York Times* that there is no profile?"

"I don't read the *Times*," Pulver said. "Profile or no profile, it's going to take a hell of a lot of basic cop work to solve this and prove who the killer is. The FBI and ATF agents are waiting in the wings to screw it up. So far it's strictly a Chicago case."

"Are there clues yet about the bomb itself?" I asked. "Can't they tell what kind it was and where it was bought and that kind of stuff from the remnants?"

"It was probably ammonium nitrate and fertilizer. Lots of it."

I nodded, thought for a minute, then asked, "Am I in danger?"

"Maybe. Kenny says he recommended twenty-four-hour security."

"Yeah, but what the hell am I supposed to do for the rest of my life? What do the cops advise? Hiding here for the next decade?"

"You've got tough choices to make," Pulver said.

"What about hiring my own investigator on this thing?"

"I don't see how that will help," Pulver said, "and you've already got the security firm."

"They give security." I turned to McCutcheon. "You going to investigate this?"

"We're licensed for it, but we don't have anywhere near the manpower. We're a small firm with only a few select clients to protect. To bust an international spy ring you need the CIA, not a security firm."

"Police won't like someone sticking their nose in this," Pulver said. "I wouldn't. They especially won't like it if they find out I'm giving information."

"Why would I tattle on somebody who's helping me out? Why would you have told me this stuff if you didn't think I could keep my mouth shut?"

"I like you. I admire your guts. And Kenny vouched for you."

I stood up and walked to the windows. No insight leapt into the room.

"I'm going to see Tom." I turned to them. "I appreciate the information you've given me. I feel a little more in control, even though I know I'm not."

"If I can help with anything," Pulver said, "call me." He left.

McCutcheon said he would accompany me to the hospital along with one of his other guards. We drove over with Oscar Hills, a former hockey player who had just missed getting into the National Hockey League because of a conviction for battery in Alberta, Canada. Complicating his case was that the person he'd attacked had been his coach. He was short and stocky and one of the few guys McCutcheon had with a little bit of a sense of humor.

"Pulver called you Kenny," I said while we were stopped at Clark Street and North Avenue.

"Yes, I know" was McCutcheon's entire answer.

8

At the hospital Tom was still in intensive care. They had done a CAT scan and there was no internal bleeding. The diagnosis was that he had a severe concussion and would wake up when he would—probably sooner rather than later. The inability of medical personnel to be definitive pisses me off, as it does everybody else. And like most people, I realize they can't say for sure. Definite answers lead to lawsuits and, worse, crushed expectations. One prof I had in college said that revolutions aren't caused as people are driven steadily into despair. They are caused when the expectations of the people are raised, then dashed. At least medically I can understand how that can be true.

Tom's dad and two of his brothers were there. When I arrived, they went down to the lounge to get something to eat. I sat by Tom's side and held his hand. My guards waited outside. I watched the rise and fall of the sheet over Tom's chest. The IV dripped. The machines he was being monitored by hummed softly. The flowers in their vases looked pretty and kept quiet. I know Tom would say this was a good thing in an inanimate object.

I talked to Tom for a while. I didn't care if he couldn't hear. I told him I loved him and how I missed him and about things we would do when he was better. Mostly things I wanted to do that he hated. He was unconscious, so what better time to suggest a trip to Branson, Missouri? The man's dislike for twangy country music sometimes approaches the pathological.

His mother, sister, and several older nephews showed up. They sat with me. We talked in low voices. Mostly we reassured each other about how tough Tom was, and how we all had to hope for the best. I was over my funk from last night and I found their presence comforting.

Brandon Kearn showed up without a camera crew. He was in faded blue jeans and a blue, crew-neck T-shirt. "How is he?" Kearn asked.

"Not worse, but not awake."

"Not worse is good?"

"I hope so."

Kearn nodded toward McCutcheon and Oscar. "Why are there armed guards here?"

"You can tell they're guards?"

"Both of them gave me a suspicious once-over, and I'm a good reporter. I can tell if someone is armed or not."

"They're security guards I've hired." I introduced him to them.

"I've heard of you," Kearn said. "Your firm guards a lot of high-profile celebrities."

McCutcheon nodded.

Kearn and I moved away from them. "I came to see how you were doing," Kearn said, "but also to tell you I'm going to be doing some investigating."

"You're using this to become famous like Arthur Kent in the Gulf War. Last night I thought you were fed up."

"I was tired and frightened. I haven't gotten much sleep, but I know I'm in the middle of a once-in-a-lifetime opportunity, a career-maker. You should realize that too. I'd be happy to interview you."

"I've already got plenty of fame, thanks. Is that the only reason you came, to see if I could help your skyrocketing career?"

"Partly."

I guess I was glad he was being honest. "I can't be that big of a deal."

"I hear they're considering you for the cover of *People* magazine. They've got a photo of you with your arm around a fireman helping him to an ambulance."

"I don't remember flashbulbs going off."

"I've seen it. It's you."

I snorted. "If somebody had gotten a picture of a child being rescued, that would make the cover of everything. Frankly, I wish somebody had. I was just doing the right thing."

"While I'm after any edge I can get, I'm also trying to do the right thing. I've got a big story now, and I want my part to keep getting bigger. I'm going to be on *Nightline* Monday." Kearn moved closer. I could smell his cologne and coffee on his breath. He muttered, "I know it's hard to believe that a heartless, cliché-handsome reporter would care about someone who is injured, but I do. But since I am indeed a heartless, cliché reporter, I want to offer a deal. I'll funnel you the information I get. If you think it's enough to grant me an interview, will you call?"

I nodded agreement. I doubt if what he found would be that helpful to us. Kearn wished me well and left.

Morty, my catcher from the team, arrived. He hugged me and stayed for a while. The guy can be so soothing even under the toughest conditions. A few minutes after he left, the nurse came in to change Tom's IV bag and check the machines.

She rummaged in the drawer of the cabinet next to Tom's bed. She took out an empty bedpan and an envelope. "Did one of you leave this here?" She held the envelope out to me. "Isn't this your name?"

"Scott Carpenter" was typed on the outside of the envelope. I frowned and reached out for it. McCutcheon noticed the action and strolled over.

Tom's mother, sister, and McCutcheon leaned over my shoulder as I opened the envelope. Inside was a single piece of paper with one line of type all in lowercase: "you're next faggot."

Everyone who wasn't standing, leapt to their feet— except Tom of course. His sister gave a loud gasp and fainted. Before I could catch her, she tipped over a stainless-steel tray. I did manage to cushion her fall a little bit. Seconds later hospital workers crowded the doorway.

Mrs. Mason snatched the note from my hand. She glanced at it, turned it over to the blank side, then threw it to the ground. She reached for me and clutched my arm. She breathed deeply for several moments, then pulled herself up to her full height. "This has gone far enough," she stated.

I agreed.

McCutcheon carefully picked up the envelope and note and examined them. Hospital security guards showed up in minutes and the police a short while later. Moments after them, Stan Goodman, the head of hospital security, arrived. He ordered a list be compiled of the names of every person who worked on or had any kind of official access to this floor.

"What about strangers?" McCutcheon asked.

"Wouldn't someone have noticed a stranger?" I asked.

"This isn't a closed floor," Goodman said. "People aren't supposed to just walk around aimlessly, but it happens. A determined killer with a thought-out scheme could probably get away with more than I'd care to admit."

While hospital workers scrambled about, I fumed and fretted. The string of possible coincidences was too long already to think that Tom just happened to be in the hospital where a mass murderer worked. However, three facts were incontrovertible: the threat to me on the street, the bomb in his truck, and now this piece of paper. In my mind the idea that somebody had specifically targeted him and me was unquestionable. Whether it had anything to do with the massive devastation yesterday was still open to doubt.

McCutcheon said little. Mrs. Mason quietly but firmly demanded a complete investigation. We were all promised this would happen. I also insisted we call Larry Jantoro, the detective who had questioned me the night before.

Half an hour later, Mrs. Mason, McCutcheon, Jantoro, and I were ushered into Norton Smithers's office on the twelfth floor. Smithers, the head administrator of the hospital, was a white-haired man in his early sixties. Stan Goodman joined us. He briefed Smithers on everything that had been done so far.

Jantoro said, "We'll need the names of all the personnel who worked on that floor."

"It's being compiled," Goodman said.

Jantoro asked, "Any reports of strangers?"

Smithers said, "There are other people on that floor who have had visitors. We hardly dare intrude on their grief by asking them to name names. Do you really think a killer would be able to put someone on that floor at that time just to make a threat against another patient?"

"Logistically a nightmare," Goodman said.

"But Mr. Mason himself had visitors," Smithers said. "Shouldn't we have a list of those?"

I said, "Nobody who came to visit Tom would make threats against him."

"They had the easiest access to his room," Goodman said. "We should check them out."

"We can't have our own family investigated," Mrs. Mason said. "You need to start with hospital personnel."

Smithers said, "They will be as resentful of police intrusion as would your family."

"We need to examine everyone," Jantoro said.

"The investigation has barely had time to begin," Goodman said. "We promise to be very unintrusive but very thorough. We're still checking personnel records for anything out of line."

I asked, "A killer is going to put that kind of thing on an application?"

"Don't you do background checks?" Mrs. Mason asked.

Smithers said, "If a madman hasn't been arrested before, he or she wouldn't have a record that shows up in such a check."

Jantoro said, "The police will have to talk to everybody on that floor. We'll run their names through the police computers and see if anything turns up. In the normal course of events, we wouldn't think much of a threat like this."

"Why not?" Mrs. Mason asked.

"Mr. Carpenter has received thousands of threats," Jantoro said.

"Not this close or this direct," I said. "In a place hard to get to. Done like this, it was designed specifically for maximum shock."

Jantoro continued, "But because of its connection to the bombing, we're going to give it more than usual consideration. I doubt if it had much to do with the explosions, but it is another anomaly and we've got to check it out."

I said, "I'd like to be there for the interviews of the hospital employees."

"Impossible," Jantoro said.

Mrs. Mason said, "I'm incredibly frightened, incredibly angry, and nearly out of my mind with worry about my son. I have a right to—"

I put my hand on her arm and said, "What I really want to do is help. Maybe one of us could just sit in. I'd be very quiet. In the background."

"You'd be recognized," Jantoro said. "I assume people on that floor already know who you are. What we'd get is a circus atmosphere. A recognized public figure who just happens to be sitting in on an interrogation could raise all kinds of questions."

I began a protest, but Jantoro interrupted, "I understand you're upset, but we'll handle it. It's what we're trained to do. We care as much as you do about solving this."

I asked, "By *this,* do you mean the bombing or who's been making these threats?"

"Both," Jantoro said.

"Shouldn't there be a police guard on Mr. Mason's room?" Smithers asked.

I said, "I'll want somebody from the security firm present at all times."

McCutcheon nodded. "Oscar's down there now. I'll arrange for a twenty-four-hour-a-day rotation."

"A uniformed police officer might have a strong detrimental effect as well," Smithers said.

"That won't be a problem," Jantoro said. "Although, you do realize, that if someone wanted to murder Mr. Mason, he or she could have killed him when they were placing the note in the drawer."

"Wouldn't there have been witnesses?" I asked.

"You'd think there would have been to whoever put the note in," Jantoro said. "Since no one saw the person place the note in the drawer, I think a possible assumption is there was no witness and if they wanted to kill him, they could have."

We sat in appalled silence and digested this information. I realized what Jantoro had said was obvious. I should have thought of it.

Mrs. Mason said, "You're right. I think they wanted to frighten us. They've succeeded with me. If they wanted to kill him, they would have."

Other gay people had paid a higher price for being open than Tom or I had so far. I felt guilt because Tom wouldn't be in danger if he didn't know me. Maybe they'd kill him to get at me. Killing someone isn't always the most vicious revenge—making people suffer a grievous loss for the rest of their life insures getting even to the greatest degree.

My frustration had continued to build. Hiring guards and police protection seemed purely defensive. Between Tom and me, I'm almost always the more cautious one. If there's a hesitation to be had, I'll think of it. It's not that Tom's particularly hotheaded, it's just that I've usually found that proceeding cautiously is more effective than rushing off blindly. But I was really upset and frustrated. The police wanted me out of their way, but I had to do something to make it seem as if I weren't simply being overwhelmed by circumstances beyond my control. I thought several moments, then announced, "I'm hiring a private investigator."

"You think that will help?" Mrs. Mason asked.

"If I hire someone, I'll feel like I'm taking positive action. The police don't want us interfering, but I can still do something." I looked at McCutcheon.

He said, "I think the police have a lot more chance of finding anything out. They have files, background, computers, and especially personnel who can question people, take notes, write reports, coordinate efforts." He shrugged. "But you can spend your money any way you want."

Jantoro said, "Any outside interference will be frowned on."

"I'm going to do something," I stated. "You won't let me be at the interviews. Fine. I'll hire my own interviewer. I'll hire an entire goddamn agency if I want to."

No one denied me my right to be inflexibly stubborn or my right to spend my money in a possibly useless activity. My innate caution had given way to frustration, anger, and fear. Our discussion finished, Mrs. Mason and I returned to Tom's room.

I was tired. I was working on only three hours of sleep. I felt out of control, unreasonable, and irrationally stubborn. The note had me shaken. Every time I thought about it, I began to tremble. I wasn't sure whether this was from rage or fear; probably both. Calm in the face of chaos wasn't new to me, but I was closer to the edge now than I'd ever been while pitching. Throwing baseballs was a job. This was personal.

◣ 9 ◢

Two hours later I was in the offices of Borini and Faslo, the largest, most sought after, and most prestigious firm of private detectives in the city. Their offices covered the entire twenty-second and twenty-third floors of the Sears Tower.

I'd asked McCutcheon for a recommendation. Like me, he only knew of Borini and Faslo by reputation. They had been on the cover of *Chicago* magazine and had had flattering profiles in the *Sun-Times, Tribune,* and *Daily Herald.* Their first notoriety had come when they'd gotten banner headlines while uncovering dirt in a divorce case between a pro hockey player and his wife, a messy affair involving custody warfare over three kids under the age of six, millions of dollars, a mistress for him, and a gigolo for her.

My fame had gotten us an appointment with Frank Borini and Daniel Faslo late on a Sunday afternoon. Their offices were furnished mostly with gargantuan plants, and strips of chrome outlining every flat surface. It struck me as sort of a rain forest in chains. The only other person I saw was in a distant office—a man in his twenties typing rapidly.

Borini was slightly over six feet tall and looked to be in his early forties. He combed the remaining strands of his heavily greased hair straight back from his forehead. Faslo was around five-eight. He kept the remaining strands on his nearly bald head cut short in bold assertion of a military-style brush cut. Both wore dark gray suits.

We sat on cherry-colored leather chairs around an oak coffee table. After everyone was comfortable, I said, "I want to hire you to investigate who blew up the block on the North Side and to find out who's making threats against my lover and me." I gave them details.

They waited until I finished, then smiled indulgently. "You're joking," Borini said.

I didn't smile. "No."

Their smiles faded. Faslo asked, "Do you understand the impossibility of a private firm trying such an undertaking?"

"I hire you. You investigate. What's the problem?"

I saw Faslo biting back another smile. He said, "We are not mini–James Bonds here. We do divorce work and domestic surveillance. We investigate industrial sabotage and computer crimes. We help in numerous extremely complicated court cases. Nobody here carries a gun. We don't have access to police, FBI, or ATF files. They're the ones you should go to."

I reiterated my anxiety about the personal nature of the attacks.

"You've told all this to the police?" Faslo asked.

I nodded.

Borini said, "I appreciate your concern and the nature of your involvement, but, really, the official government agencies should be the ones to handle it. We don't have the resources. We are not an international-terrorist fighting organization and we don't want to be. We don't have exotic lone-wolf detectives with machine guns and a penchant for violence. That's television, not reality. And what if we got a reputation for hunting terrorists? Then wouldn't we become targets ourselves? I think so."

"I will pay you a million dollars—half now and half when you find out who has been making these threats, and a five-hundred-thousand-dollar bonus if they go to prison."

That stopped them. Normally, I hate flashing my money around. See, there's this thing I've learned about being fabulously wealthy. People generally pay some kind of attention. Not only am I paid millions as a baseball player, but before the sexual-orientation publicity, I made almost as much money from endorsements as Michael Jordan does. I've saved my money and put it in nice conservative, steady moneymaking investments. Basically, I'm still a kid from a rural farm in the South and reasonably shy. I know that might be hard to believe about a famous athlete, but it's true. For the first few years the money kind of turned my head, but not anymore. The number of those dopey "collectible" figurines I bought years ago in airports around the country is embarrassing. And Tom is good at bringing me back to reality. Nothing like being filthy rich and your boyfriend telling you that your teeth need brushing before making love. But if I've got that much money, why shouldn't I use it at a moment like this?

Faslo asked, "You're willing to spend that kind of money on just the threats, not the bombing?"

"If the two are connected, both."

"It's a lot of money," Borini said.

"Why didn't you have someone investigate the threats before?" Faslo asked. "You must have reported it to the police."

"The police did investigate. They got nothing. I thought there was no more to be done. Now, I want to try you guys." I sat forward. "Look, I just want to protect myself as much as possible. The security guards are one thing, but that's mostly defensive. If I hire investigators, I feel like I'm doing something, taking some action."

"You realize," Faslo said, "that it is extremely unlikely that we would find out anything that the police haven't? While I'd hate to pass up a massive fee, really, we are not the ones you should go to."

"I can find another agency."

"Yes, you'll probably find someone to take your money. They may even lie about how effective they will be." Faslo shrugged. "I can't prevent that."

"What about the note at the hospital?" I asked. "You must be able to ask questions about that."

Faslo said, "I need to talk to my partner for a few moments." They rose and left the room.

"I wish I knew more about these guys," McCutcheon said.

"You want me to have you investigate the investigators?"

"Lot of that going around these days. Might not hurt for me to make a few more calls. Having a reputation is one thing. Knowing their real background is another."

After fifteen minutes Borini and Faslo reentered the room. Borini said, "The police are better equipped to do any investigating in what is undoubtedly a complex matter. However, if you give us a retainer of fifty thousand dollars, we will commit resources to finding out who has been threatening you. Obviously this will include asking questions at the hospital about the note. We will not directly involve ourselves in the bombing investigation. As we said, even if we cared to, we do not have the resources for such an undertaking. We promise to follow up every lead we get. As long as you understand, Mr. Carpenter, that we guarantee nothing. That if we come up with any information about the bombing, we will be giving it to the police as well as you. It is most likely that we will come up with nothing. Your offer of a million dollars is out of line. I hate to let it go. At the moment we'll take the much lesser amount. As I'm sure you know, money is not always the answer, nor is greed. Who knows, we might get prestige from having Scott Carpenter as a client."

"I want to be there when you ask questions at the hospital."

"No," Borini said. "You are hiring us because we're professionals. We know our business. You would be in the way."

"I'm the client."

"And you're rich," Borini said. "We know that, but we're going to do this our way."

"I guess you will." They weren't giving me a lot of choices. So much for throwing my money around to get instant gratification. Tom would advise me to stick with chocolate to fill this latter need.

We left. It was after six. The Loop was nearly deserted of traffic. The weather continued perfect. The sunset was golden orange, soft pinks, and soothing blues. The enjoyable warmth of the day was fading to a pleasantly cool evening. I slumped in the passenger seat of McCutcheon's Hummer. Several times I almost nodded off as we drove to the hospital.

The last streaks of sunset hung in the sky as I talked to the doctor and Tom's family outside his room. There had been no change in his condition.

.10.

The first thing I noticed when I woke up was dull pain all over, and a feeling that I'd been drugged. I noted that I was in a bed, and I was looking out a window at the end of a sunset or the beginning of a sunrise. I heard the murmur of voices at some distance. I wondered why an IV tube was attached to my arm. I shut my eyes and slept.

11

McCutcheon drove me home.

I phoned Tom's school number for substitute teachers and left a message on the machine. I called several of Tom's close friends from work to give them the news.

In the living room I turned on the stereo system and then shut off all the lights. I let the glow from the city outside and the digital readout on the stereo illumine the white carpet and the white furniture. I picked out a tape I'd made from all my county-and-western CDs. It consisted of the softest ballads and the most melancholy and sappy songs of the past thirty years. The best part was all of Mary Chapin Carpenter's slow songs at the start of the first side of the tape. Even Tom likes those. I rewound it to the beginning. I lay on the couch and let her voice soothe me. I did my best to suppress the still undimmed memories of the carnage I'd seen. My exhaustion finally overcame my swirling thoughts. The last song I remembered was Lyle Lovett singing "Step Inside This House."

I woke in the living room to full morning. I called the hospital. They thought Tom was sleeping and not in a coma anymore. I showered, dressed, and called security. McCutcheon picked me up, and we hurried over. Tom wasn't awake, but the doctors were hopeful.

About nine, one of Tom's friends, a drag queen named Myrtle Mae Zagglioni, swept in. Myrtle Mae was known to a few of us as Bryce Bennet, scion to an agribusiness fortune. Myrtle Mae would rather lose his entire wardrobe than have this fact broadcast. The way I heard the story was that ever since he'd run away from home when he was sixteen, Myrtle Mae had tried to live down his wealthy background. When he was young, he supposedly lived a raucous and exciting life: driving a garbage truck in New York for a while; being thrown out of the Peace Corps for radical activities in South America; and picking grapes in California with the United Farm Workers, an avocation particularly offensive to his family. How much of any of these and more were true, I didn't know. Tom wasn't sure and claimed he was too discreet to ask. I thought this was a crock. Tom loves gossip as much as the most notorious queeny Hollywood reporter, he just hates to admit it. I know better. I think he just hadn't found anybody who was willing to tell.

With Myrtle Mae was his sometime companion John Werner. He was in his late sixties or early seventies. Werner always dressed in pastel colors or washed-out grays. He seldom spoke. With Myrtle Mae, if you looked beyond the layers of makeup and the glitter to the lines around his eyes and the wattles he tried to cover over, you could tell he had to be near Werner's age. It was rumored that they had once been lovers. While they did not live together, Werner accompanied Myrtle Mae to weddings, funerals, and I guessed now, hospital visits.

Werner I didn't mind. I disliked Myrtle Mae intensely. As far as I knew, he never appeared outside of drag. I don't mind drag, but like most gay people it irritates me that the straight media usually shows only pictures of drag queens after every gay pride parade. I am unable to explain, and I'm not sure anyone can, the endless fascination the straight media have with drag queens. I hesitate to embrace the theory that this emphasis comes about because drag is seen as the safe way to deal with gay people. The semitragic, overemotional, clownish buffoon as role model? As acceptable icon? Think Amos and Andy in the fifties and how offensive that is today. I believe the prevalence of drag portrayals is a way to keep us marginalized, to keep prominent the message to the silly and righteously Christian that drag is all that gay people are. That we are as pathetic if occasionally amusing as most drag queens are portrayed.

Unfortunately, the straight media's interest in the drag-queen phenomenon is only slightly greater than that shown by the gay media. I don't understand that either. Don't get me wrong. I have a soft spot for drag queens, as I suspect all gay people do, because of their role in the Stonewall riots. Plus, I don't mind if people want to do drag, but dressing up, costumes, and exaggerated effeminacy are not my thing. What can I say? I flunked Halloween as a kid.

The real reason I can't stand Myrtle Mae, though, is his condescending attitude toward me. I'm sorry that he was picked on by the more coordinated and athletic of his class-mates in school. I had nothing to do with it. He always man-ages to make some snide crack about my being a jock, usually connecting the comment with a vicious swipe at my IQ level. Lots of gay people look down on me because I'm a jock. Even worse, I don't like opera, don't know the name of the trend-iest art galleries in New York, and don't know the names of very many long-dead actresses. Nor do I particularly care to change their notions about me. I'm comfortable with who I am. The truth is, I graduated summa cum laude from college. Yeah, my major was PE, but I minored in both philosophy and math. I liked the logic of them. I would be damned if I would defend myself to this or any other shallow creep by mentioning these facts. Tom knows how I feel about Myrtle Mae. I won't let Tom tell about my college record either. On the other hand, I have also discovered that a college degree is no defense against stupidity.

This morning Myrtle Mae's impressive bulk was en-shrouded in pink chiffon, which barely hid his jiggling flab. I could picture him eating himself to death, a dead drag queen on a heap of candy wrappers, and felt immediate guilt for this thought.

In deference to the slight cooling from yesterday, Myrtle Mae wore a fur wrap. He often proclaimed he did this delib-erately to annoy the pro-pet, anti-fur crowd.

He said, "I saw on the news that Tom was injured. I watched every bit of coverage from the moment it came on until early this morning." He glanced through the doorway at Tom's sleeping figure. "Will he survive?"

"They think so," I said.

After I gave him an update, he commented, "Well, darling, they're using all that medical jargon, are you sure you can keep up?"

"About as well as your tits do."

I'm not sure hate encompasses how I feel about him. The best example I can think of to describe his personality is this: Myrtle Mae/Bryce Bennet was the kind of person people got caller ID for so they could avoid their calls. He mixed vicious, cold asperity with cloyingly sweet attempts at intimacy. He was the kind who often greeted friends with "Why haven't you called me?" The mostly unstated response to this question was "Because you're a jerk." For reasons I was unable to fathom, Myrtle Mae got on famously with Tom's mother and father.

Myrtle Mae clutched the pearls around his throat and exclaimed dramatically, "I'll have you know I was one of the fortunate ones. I was eating at Fattatuchi's Deli earlier that evening. I had to have one of their triple-decker chocolate cakes for a party I was throwing, and as long as I was there, I thought I could eat a piece of one of those luscious confections in the display case just to tide me over. Fortunately, I was long gone before the explosion."

"Have you talked to the police?" I asked.

"Should I? If I do, I want a burly, masculine one, with dark stubble all over his chin, and he should be wearing a dark, dark blue uniform, starched and ironed within an inch of its life."

"You'll probably get a plainclothes detective."

"You're always so dull."

"Did you see anything suspicious that night?"

"The Fattatuchis are absolutely the most dear friends of mine. I've actually eaten there innumerable times over the years. I haven't had to pay for a meal since 1982. We exchange Christmas gifts. I'm the godfather of one of their grandchildren."

Count on Myrtle Mae to claim to be best friends with two of the most popular restaurant owners in Chicago. He often intimated that he knew people who knew people who knew where secrets were kept and bodies were buried. I didn't believe most of it.

Fattatuchi's Deli had morphed over the years into one of

the most popular restaurants and bakeries in the city.

Myrtle Mae said, "Mr. and Mrs. Fattatuchi were having some kind of quarrel, but aren't they always? Half the draw of the place is to watch the Fattatuchi family soap opera play out before our very eyes. They spent most of the time arguing with their son, who is not very tall really, but blade thin. He was wearing a black leather vest, tight black jeans, a black T-shirt, and sunglasses."

"Indoors at night?" I asked.

"If he was suspicious, he was a cliché. No one runs around looking like a terrorist, do they? Besides, he was a local and worth every stare. I could spend hours just watching him breathe."

"What you mean is you saw nothing you considered suspicious."

"Correct."

I wanted the annoying old queen to leave, but I couldn't think of a polite way of telling him to do so. Much as I hated the idea, he was Tom's friend, and I could at least try to be civil. And if I was nice, I would certainly rack up moral-superiority points. If one is going to have fun in life, it's always good to be ahead on moral-superiority points. It's not quite as good as having more toys than anyone else when you die, but it's close. And there is nothing like having the moral high ground when dealing with an annoying old queen. It may not be much, but it's something.

"Did the Fattatuchis survive the blast?" I asked.

"Mrs. Fattatuchi is fine. Mr. Fattatuchi is in the hospital, but will make a full recovery." Myrtle Mae placed a manicured fist on his left hip and leaned toward me. "Why aren't you doing something about this? If Tom was conscious, he'd be out investigating. I have contacts. I could help him."

"Why? Are you a terrorist bomber?"

"You can't be involved in activist causes for forty years and not know things."

I didn't for a minute believe he had any contacts. I figured he was overemphasizing his importance. A habit of his that he'd turned into a lifestyle.

Myrtle Mae said, "Tom'd know where to start, which places to go, and to whom he should talk. I think—"

Werner spoke for the first time since we'd exchanged greetings. "Bryce, you're going too far. Stop it." Myrtle Mae flashed him an annoyed look, but he did not complete his thought.

I wanted to slap the moronic twit silly. He was such a consummate know-it-all. He enjoyed pretending he was on more intimate terms with Tom than I was. Why he and Tom remained friends, I'm not sure. Tom gets kind of vague about their background, and I don't pry. Sometimes I wonder if maybe Myrtle Mae has pictures of Tom naked in bed with a woman or something equally outré.

However, Mrs. Mason was nearby, and I didn't want a scene in the hospital. I whispered, "I don't feel any need to justify myself to you, Myrtle Mae, but I have hired the firm of Borini and Faslo to investigate." And I hated myself instantly for that brief bit of self-justification.

"You hired Borini and Faslo? You nitwit. That firm and those two in particular are the most homophobic, right-wing, narrow-minded assholes in the city. One of their prime targets is finding closeted gay men and putting pressure on them to stay married to their wives. Rumor is that they are tools of the religious right, that they are in thick with the gay-conversion people, if not actually funding part of the ex-gay movement."

"They seemed perfectly professional to me."

"They would. I wish Tom were awake to hear this."

That did it. I pushed my face three inches from his. "Get out," I ordered softly. "I don't want you around here. I don't care how good a friend you are with Tom or his parents. I will personally escort you out in five seconds if you don't get your underdressed ass out of here."

"Brute," he snarled. Then Myrtle Mae harrumphed dramatically, eyed the others down the corridor, made a sweeping 180-degree turn, adjusted his fur, and marched away. At the elevator he waited until the door binged open, then he turned around, sneered at me, and called, "A stupid jock like you will ruin everything."

Werner took one of Myrtle Mae's elbows and dragged him into the elevator.

Several people heard the commotion and turned to stare. I vowed we would never see the overbearing creep socially again.

I walked over to McCutcheon and told him about the possible homophobia at Borini and Faslo.

"Did you ask him how he knew?" McCutcheon asked.

"No."

"That bit of information would be important and an obvious place to begin asking questions."

"I was too angry to think of anything besides getting him out of here. Did you think they were homophobic?"

"Everyone in the city knows who you and Tom are. They gave no indication that they cared you and he are lovers. I called a contact. He didn't mention anything about homophobia."

"Maybe your contact isn't gay and wouldn't necessarily be aware of any prejudice. Everybody sees the positive articles about that firm. Who's to know the real story?"

"I'll try a couple more calls." McCutcheon pulled out his portable phone and moved off a few feet.

While he was on the phone, a nurse in her sixties entered. She held out a box full of pink phone message slips to Tom's mother and me. "These have been accumulating downstairs." We'd had all the calls to this room stopped at the switchboard.

I riffled through them. Many were from friends of Tom's wishing him well. A fistful were from reporters. None of them read "you're next faggot." One was from Brandon Kearn asking me to call and saying it was urgent.

I used the phone in Tom's room to call the television station. They paged Kearn. He called back in five minutes.

"Who's in the room with you?" he asked. "Can they hear you?"

"Just about everybody can hear me."

Mrs. Mason gave me an odd look.

Kearn said, "I've got some information that could be vital to you, but I need to see you without anyone else around."

"Couldn't you come here? We could walk down the hall to an empty room."

"I've got some information about the crime as well. I'm calling you from the scene. You're in more danger than you imagine."

"There's no need to be melodramatic. Why not just tell me what you've got?"

"My suggestion would be that you tell no one that you are coming to talk to me."

"Do you really think I could do that with all that's happened to me?"

"You've known me from before all this."

"We're not friends."

"At some point you're going to have to trust someone."

"Not necessarily."

"Look, meet me here, alone, or not at all. I believe it is in your own best interest to tell no one. I figured you'd be interested in what I have to say, but it's your choice."

"Maybe you're just trying to get me alone and unprotected."

"Believe me or not. I'll be here for at least another half an hour. You decide." Kearn hung up.

12

This was a hell of a choice. Feeling conflicted like that drives me nuts. I sort of wanted to investigate. I certainly wanted the threats to stop. I mostly wanted Tom to get better. My innate caution told me not to go to such a meeting without security. If I did so, I'd have to explain to McCutcheon that I was leaving without protection. Was having this kind of security turning out to be as much albatross as salvation? I hadn't thought of my defensive measures as a wall that would keep me in as well as a barrier to keep others away. As a necessary evil, sure, but now I wondered, if I wanted to be free of him, how I could accomplish it if I chose to be so? I could just say, I'm an adult, I've made a decision, and I'm leaving, but even that had consequences. I could sneak out, but I wasn't some teenager in an unrealistic television show trying to get a laugh from a preprogrammed sound track. I could always try simple, straightforward honesty. Kearn was the one who thought there was a need for secrecy.

I said to McCutcheon and Mrs. Mason, "That was Brandon Kearn. He says he has some information to tell me, but he wants to see me alone."

"Why alone?" McCutcheon asked.

"All he said was that it was important that I come by myself."

"Can you trust him?" Mrs. Mason asked.

"How could it be a trap if I've told everyone I'm going? You both know who called and where I'm headed. How would he have the nerve to try something? He'd be the obvious suspect."

"You can broadcast to the world it's a trap," Mrs. Mason said, "but if you go anyway, it's still a trap."

"Why don't I have one of my people follow at a discreet distance?" McCutcheon said. "For that matter, why can't he come here and tell you what he claims is important?"

This was awful quick to be dropping the concept of twenty-four-hour-a-day security. Then again, assuming Kearn was trustworthy, could I presume that a killer and possible mass murderer hadn't had the time to sit in a parking lot waiting for me to wander out alone? Then again, someone had found his way into this hospital room.

Between Tom and me I'm always the more reluctant. The one who says wait, let's think about it and consider all the options. Neither the police nor Faslo and Borini wanted me around to help investigate or ask questions. Here was something I could do.

"I'll call in every half hour," I said.

"Big help," McCutcheon said. "In half a second you could be dead."

"At least let one of the security guards follow you," Mrs. Mason said. "All that's happened has been too dangerous and too bizarre to take chances. If Kearn poses a danger, you could tell him you came alone. How would he know every person in the security firm? Obviously he wouldn't. Have the guard get out of the car a block away from the meeting place. He can follow you."

This made sense. Oscar Hills, the guard, accompanied me. In the car I explained about parking at a distance and his following me.

Hills said, "I'm not the one in danger. I know my job and how to keep out of sight. Do you know yours?"

"I'm not sure what my job is. I'm just trying to make some pain go away."

The scene of the explosion had been converted into orderly chaos. Investigators moved methodically through the ruins near me, and farther away backhoes and cranes rumbled over the mountains of debris. A large parking lot across from the remains of the clinic had hundreds of tagged parts all arranged in a circle. I saw people sifting through debris. Some were carting away large vats filled with rubble. I saw people using rakes to hunt through the mess, looking for the tiniest fragments that would give them clues to how the crime had been done and by whom.

To hunt for Kearn, I walked around the perimeter of the area roped off by the crime-scene tape. Chicago cops stood guard to keep the crowd of onlookers from intruding on the investigation. I forced myself to stop looking around to see where Oscar was.

The day was pleasantly cool with a slight breeze from the north hinting more of winter to come than of summer past. I asked several people if they had seen Kearn, but no one had. No one thrust his curiosity in my face about who I was, either. From under the el across from a burned-out police car, I saw the top of a well-coiffed head, the hair looking cemented in place. This area was fairly deserted and protected from the eyes of the other workers by a wall of fire-blackened brick. I called Kearn's name. Along with another man I didn't know, he scrambled out of the hole he'd been in. They ducked under the crime-scene tape and strode over to me. Kearn said, "Glad you came. This is Jack Wolf. He's an official investigator for the fire department."

Wolf was about six foot three with light brown hair. Maybe in his midthirties, freckles in a swath over his nose, and steel-gray eyes.

"I can't be seen with you two." Wolf turned to Kearn. "I got you past the police lines. That's all I can do for now. We'll have to talk later, if at all." Wolf hurried off.

"What was that all about?" I asked.

"He knows details about the investigation that might be important."

"Has he told them to you?"

"He's told me some. I think he wants to tell me more. I mentioned I knew you. I think he wants to give information to you."

"Why me?"

"I get the impression he's sympathetic to you as a gay man."

"He's gay?"

"He didn't say so, but I presumed so."

"What is it you wanted to tell me?" I asked.

"Couple things. First, I heard you hired a private investigating firm."

"Yeah, I hired Borini and Faslo. I haven't found out anything from them yet." I told him about the threat in the hospital.

"They're supposed to be the best," Kearn said, "but didn't I hear a rumor that they were homophobic? Wasn't there some kind of lawsuit from a former employee?"

"I never heard about it." Bitchiness from a dizzy drag queen I could ignore. The same information coming from Kearn made it begin to sound as if I'd made a mistake.

Kearn said, "I've found out a few things, some of which relate more to you and your lover than the bombing itself. I've been asking a lot of questions." He glanced around the street. "You didn't bring anyone with you?"

"You told me not to."

"Let's find someplace quiet."

"I'd rather not go anyplace far with you."

"You don't trust me?"

"Is there a rule book on who I should and should not trust?"

"There's a coffee shop halfway down the next block. We can talk there. It's open. It's public."

I could only be so churlish and suspicious. Besides, I had a tail. It was broad daylight with hundreds of people around.

On our way to the shop, I said, "Why are you doing this for me and why does it have to be so secret?"

"I'm doing it because I feel sorry for you and your lover. Because I think you need to know some of the information. The danger you are in is more pervasive than you can imagine. Plus, if what I know turns out to be accurate, I'd have another big story. As you know, you are news."

We entered the coffee shop. We wound up in the back booth of a café that Edward Hopper could have used for a model. The waitress filled our coffee cups and took our orders. Kearn wrapped his fingers around the porcelain and murmured, "I think I've slept two whole hours since the bombing." He sipped coffee.

I said, "My nightmares have all been filled with burning bodies running and screaming down the streets of Chicago.

Often they are worse than my waking memories, but not by much."

Kearn nodded. "I don't look forward to trying to fall asleep again. Those few hours were bad enough. I keep pushing myself harder and harder. I try not to think. My unrealistic hope is that by the time I'm ready to try to sleep again, I'll be too tired to remember. Maybe it goes away with time."

"I sure as hell hope so."

Kearn's shoulders slumped. "I've been on seven major news shows, given more interviews than I can count, and had some big offers from national news outlets." He shook his head. "I'm not sure being a hero reporter is worth it."

"How so?"

"You were at the bomb site. You were helping the injured, like I was. You know what it's like."

I didn't remind him that I was helping long before he was. Recriminations were pointless, and I did know how he felt. "Right after the explosion you were ready to quit. Then you were on the path to fame and fortune. Now you're into fear and pointing fingers."

"I've got a big ego and a conscience. I'd like to keep both. Maybe I can have my principles and be at the top of my profession. I won't know until I'm at the top."

After our food arrived, he said, "Are Faslo and Borini officially investigating the bombing?"

"Not specifically."

"I can use anything you get from them. While I'm the flavor of the month at the moment, I want more. Most of the rest of the reporters are simply attending official press conferences and asking silly, repetitive questions. You'll share if they give you anything?"

"Sure." I was ready to go along for now.

"One of the things I heard was about the head of your

security firm, Ken McCutcheon. Do you know anything about his background?"

"Lots of rumors." I told him the ones I'd heard.

"I think the parts about him being a mercenary in Bosnia and Africa might be true. In Bosnia he was not fighting on the side of truth and light."

"How do you know?"

"He was on the side that was doing the ethnic cleansing."

"That's impossible. He's so young. He seems so normal."

"So did the Germans who worked at the concentration camps."

"Do you have proof of this? Who's your source?"

"I don't reveal sources."

"Don't give me that. I'm not an investigating government body. I'm also not somebody who is inclined to believe you. I've got to have some basis for believing what you tell me."

"I can tell you this much. It's another reporter who covered Bosnia for the networks. There are a lot of national news reporters in town to cover this. My source saw him on one of the newscasts of the bombing of your lover's truck. He called and asked me if I knew who he was."

"He could have seen him for only a few seconds. Is he sure it's the same guy?"

"He was reasonably sure. The reporter wanted to know if you guys were connected to right-wing militia groups."

"That's ludicrous."

"We check everything. I told him I didn't think gay people and right-wing militias resonated. This guy was more interested in seeing if McCutcheon could have been connected to the bombing itself. I'm interested in that, but also in finding out if he's a danger to you."

"I don't want him working for me if he was what you say, but it's going to take some convincing to prove McCutcheon is a threat to me. I'm not sure I'm ready to believe the say-so of one reporter who I've never met. It's a stretch from him maybe being in Bosnia to me being worried about him as a danger. Forgetting the international complications for a moment, if he wanted to kill me, he's had plenty of chances."

"Maybe he doesn't want to himself, but maybe he'd be willing to let someone else capitalize on the opportunity."

"Then why hasn't it happened yet?"

"It's just something I think you should be aware of. Like the guy who followed us here, who is studiously ignoring us while he sits alone in the front booth. Is it one of your security people?"

I resisted looking over my shoulder. "You exacted a promise of silence that made no sense to me. I still think you could have just come to the hospital and gone off with me quietly. Maybe you've seen too many conspiracy movies."

"Maybe you haven't seen enough. Maybe I didn't want to take the time, or I didn't have the time. Maybe I thought you'd be interested. You should have come alone. You've probably compromised me. If it's not one of your guys, we better wait here until you send for help."

I glanced around. It was Oscar. "It's one of mine. How could his presence compromise you?"

"Since he's from McCutcheon's firm, he may be a danger to you. If he's a danger to you, he might become a danger to me."

"Why? He couldn't have heard what you said. And how would his knowing you compromise you? For all he knows, maybe we're meeting to plan a clandestine love affair."

"Not if you already told McCutcheon you were meeting me. If I'm right, and they have ways of learning things, they would know where you got this information."

"Look, this is way too Byzantine. The evil guys instantly knowing the good guy's every movement and every thought until the last ten minutes before the end only happens in the movies. Your source is going to have to do better than vague fears about McCutcheon. Does your guy have pictures of McCutcheon beating up gay people? Or pictures of him standing in front of a prominent Bosnian landmark holding a dead baby? Or a video of him machine-gunning a crowded orphanage? I gotta see proof."

"My source has started checking into McCutcheon's firm. So far he's got a rumor that this 'security firm' might be a cover for a mercenary group aligned with right-wing splinter groups."

"A rumor? That's a crock. A total, complete, and utter crock! This is too loony. How am I supposed to investigate the head of my own security firm?"

"I just pass on information. What you do with it is your business."

"I'm not going to begin leading a tabloid life."

"You already do."

That stopped me. I sipped coffee. Finally I asked, "You called me to tell me this?"

"Yes. I'm willing to talk to any possible source and check out any possible lead."

"Why should I trust you?"

"Would it help if I was gay?"

"I'm not sure what would help at this point. Tom likes to talk about great flaming dragons coming down from heaven to deliver messages at important moments. He sees more humor in that comment than I do."

"Great flaming dragons aren't going to help right now."

"What other information do you have? Has anybody

talked to the protesters who are always around outside that building? They should be suspects. I saw that Lyle Gibson on a newscast making a statement."

"I'm working on getting an interview with him."

"He'd make a great suspect along with all the other regular protesters, and the people who were at that banquet."

"I assume they are looking at everybody, which must include them. I do know none of the regular protesters were seriously hurt in the explosion."

"Could they have been warned ahead of time and moved away?"

"Anything is possible."

"What about terrorists from outside the country?"

"At the moment the police think this is homegrown terrorism, not international."

"How do they know that?"

"I don't know yet. I've been developing a few other angles. I'm digging into the background information about the director of the clinic I met when I saw you in the hospital that first night."

"What about her?"

He flipped through a notebook. "Five years ago Gloria Dellios worked at a clinic in Texas where two people were shot. Three years ago she worked at a clinic in New Mexico that was firebombed. Three other places she's worked at over the years have been targets of sabotage."

"Can you prove they weren't all coincidences?"

"The string of them is getting long enough to cause me to check her out more thoroughly."

"Nobody besides you has noticed this pattern over the years?"

"I don't know yet. She wasn't the director of any of those. She started as a nurse practitioner in 1980. About ten years ago she got into administration and has been working her way up to director."

"Someone must have noticed."

"If they have, no one I've talked to in a police organization has made the connection. The cop I talked to in Chicago promised to check on it. I called Texas and New Mexico. They report nothing suspicious about her."

"Are you saying she's a random nut or that an antiabortion group planted her in all these jobs? That's awful deep cover and tremendous long-range planning. The clinics must do background checks before they hire people."

"I would presume they do," Kearn said, "but I don't know for sure. Backgrounds can be faked. Random nuts can slip through lots of cracks."

"I don't think you've got much there. Do you really think one of those true believers could work in one of those places?"

"If they thought it was the best way to enhance their cause."

"Maybe." I wasn't convinced.

"Another thing I've got. I had one of the people at the station run down the names of the owners and tenants of all the buildings that were destroyed and those on the blocks around them. I'm going to go over it for any anomalies."

"Like what?"

"The police will probably see as much as I do, but you never know what small snippet of information will break this case." Kearn shrugged. "It's like the last grain of sand that shifts a fraction of an inch and causes the earth to quake." While taking a sip from his coffee, he nodded toward the half-filled row of counter stools. "The third guy from the door has been staring at our table for some time. You know him, or did two of your security people follow us?"

I glanced as casually as I could. When the man saw my look, he got up off his stool and approached our table. I tensed immediately.

He looked to be around fifty and about seventy-five pounds overweight. He wore a red windbreaker, a blue, crew-neck T-shirt with a pocket, and white Bermuda shorts. He poked a finger at me. "You're Scott Carpenter." He began to reach into his pocket.

Oscar was there in seconds. The man was supine on the floor in less time than that. The befuddled man looked up and held out a pen. "I wanted your autograph."

Oscar helped him up. The guy was embarrassed and pissed.

I apologized, signed the autograph, and offered to get him a baseball signed by the whole team. Finally, mollified, he waddled away.

Kearn said, "If you're going to bring protection to our meetings, then they will have to be much less obvious. And you'll have to hire a firm with better operatives. I spotted your guy within two minutes."

"Then why did you keep talking to me?"

"I want an exclusive interview. I'm looking for any angle."

I gazed at him carefully.

He continued, "I'm in a profession that is ruled by tabloid journalism, but after what I've been through, I'm not sure that should be all. I'm looking for human interest with dignity, not sensationalism. They haven't snuffed out every shred of my integrity."

I guess I wanted to believe him. More for his sake than mine. I looked at his overly coiffed hair, his professionally manicured fingers, and his perfectly cut clothes. Being clean and neat is not a sure sign of corruption or of being gay, but too many things about this guy were a little too perfect. Rolling in the mud in tattered blue jeans, worn sneakers, and a ripped T-shirt aren't qualifications for sainthood, but I know which one I trust more. He got up to leave, and I stood up with him. We shook hands.

"I'm just offering you some help," Kearn said.

"I'm interested, but I'm not sure who to trust."

"When I get information, I'll share it with you. I'd appreciate it if you'd call me when you know anything." Kearn handed me his card. "That's got my home, work, and pager number on it. Call anytime."

I got back to the hospital around six. Tom's mother was on duty. A couple of relatives were getting a bite to eat. In the next couple hours numerous people from Tom's work stopped by. Meg Swarthmore, one of his best friends at school, stayed for an hour. She filled me in on more gossip about the people at school than I ever cared to remember. She kept saying, "Be sure to tell him this when he wakes up."

I must have given an annoyed sigh at one point because she finally ran down. "I guess I'm rattling on," she said, "because I'm scared. I want him to wake up."

"I've been talking to him while he's asleep," I said. "I understand the impulse."

Edwina Jenkins, his principal, came by. I told her, even if he woke up in the next five minutes, he wouldn't be in the rest of the week. She made sympathetic noises and left as quickly as was decently allowable.

Several of our gay friends showed up around eight—they were sweet and sympathetic. Then the phone rang about eight-thirty. It was the switchboard. They said they had an urgent call from someone named Myrtle Mae. Before I could tell them to take a message, I heard him say, "It is absolutely vital that I speak to them." His drag-queen persona was on high shrill and fast-forward. Maybe for some people it's hard to say no to a drag queen on a mission, not me. I hesitated, trying to think of a polite way to tell him to shove it. Unfortunately, the operator took my silence for a yes. She put him through.

"I found something out that you might be interested in knowing, and I know Tom will be when he wakes up."

"What?" I could barely get the word through gritted teeth.

"Dr. Susan Clancey was supposed to be at the clinic." He paused as if the import of this would be readily understood by me. It wasn't.

"Who is she?" I asked.

Dramatic sigh. "You don't know?"

I didn't give him the benefit of my own dramatic sigh. "If I knew, I wouldn't have asked."

"Tom will know. Susan Clancey is notorious for performing late-term abortions. Her visit to Chicago was supposed to be kept secret for obvious reasons. If it was known she was coming to town, there would have been large demonstrations. Her presence has caused near onto pitched battles in some cities."

"But no one here knew?"

"That's what I said. However, what if that knowledge leaked out?"

"Are you sure about this information? Where did you hear it?"

"A source. Tell Tom when he wakes up. He'll know it's important."

Myrtle Mae hung up. The image of him stuffing candy bars into his mouth at last year's pride parade came into my mind. At the time I'd dared to comment that what he'd draped over himself for the day looked like a cheap bedsheet.

He claimed it was the sheerest and most expensive silk. That day a friend of ours who cared enough to count claimed Myrtle Mae had eaten at least a dozen candy bars in less than two hours. I would take Myrtle Mae as seriously as I felt necessary, which wasn't much.

I turned my attention back to the friends who were there and enjoyed them until nine o'clock, when they left, then I went down to the cafeteria to get some food.

13

When I awoke for the second time, I was looking out a darkened window. It was night. Dim light came from somewhere behind me. I felt much more alert. I realized I was hooked up to various devices. I deduced I was in a hospital. I was wearing a hospital gown, which after a woman's girdle is the most singularly demeaning garment designed by man. I hadn't owned a pair of pajamas since I was ten.

I heard distant voices. I thought I recognized Scott's and my mother's. They were murmuring low and were outside my line of vision.

I thought about calling out to them, but that seemed as if it would take too much energy. I had to piss, but didn't see a bedpan. I let that idea drift off. I tried to think back to how I got here.

The last thing I remembered before waking up the first time was working in the Human Services Clinic.

I'd just had a meeting in an upstairs office with Gayle Bennet, a woman who did not like me, did not like my being there, and did not mind making her feelings about it obvious. Unfortunately, that particular day I was trying to get a project done for my friend Alvana Redpath, and I'd promised Alvana I'd be nice to Gayle. This was important to Alvana because she was trying to date Gayle. I kept telling Alvana that I thought Gayle was straight, but Alvana was smitten.

I'd been fuming as I came back down to the basement because Gayle had been unnecessarily rude, and I had swallowed my annoyance in deference to Alvana. I'd seldom met overt hostility at the clinic, but Gayle had said something about how stupid men could be. All I was doing was clearing up the filing and trying to make the system more efficient, so that it would serve the entire clinic more effectively.

After the meeting, Alvana and her son Alan had met me in the basement. She'd just picked him up from the day-care section of the clinic. Her four-year-old was one of the few kids under the age of ten who would put up with me. Scott is better with the little ones, and he always thinks I can't handle any of them. Alan was a quiet child, more given to spending time alone with a set of blocks than in socializing with the other children. I empathized. I enjoyed spending time with him. He and I were playing a haphazard game of catch with a Nerf ball as Alvana and I talked. I remember crawling under a desk to retrieve an errant toss. After that, I vaguely recalled a loud noise and pain in my head, then nothing.

I rotated my neck, moved each arm and leg, rearranged my torso. Nothing caused any particular pain. I figured this was good. I tried to lift my head. For a few seconds it was okay. Then I got dizzy and a little nauseated. I put my head back down. I would try that again later. I didn't feel tired. I concentrated for a few moments and tried calling for Scott or for my mother. My vocal chords emitted a mild harrumph. I lifted my eyes to look around as well as moving my head without lifting it from the pillow. I couldn't see a call button. I gathered my energy and turned onto my side. The light was coming through the open door to the hallway. A few feet outside the door, Scott and my mother were talking with Ken McCutcheon, Scott's head of security.

I don't like McCutcheon. In my opinion, he is too pretty and way too young to run security for anything except a Little League team. I didn't like the way Scott had checked out his background. He'd talked to a few friends. Big deal. But that was his decision. He's the one with the most death threats. I'd wanted Scott to get security far sooner than he did.

I pulled in a deep breath. I gave a call that came out somewhere between *hey, oops,* and *huh?* The three of them turned around and hurried into the room. McCutcheon stayed near the door. Scott and my mother each sat on the bed, my mother on my right, Scott on my left. Each held a hand.

My mother said, "Tom, you're awake."

I nodded. She's good with the obvious.

"Are you all right?" she asked.

I gave it another nod. My "Yes" came out as "Yumphs."

Scott said, "You've been unconscious for two days. The doctor says nothing is broken, and they don't think anything is damaged permanently."

"We should get the doctor in here," my mother said. "At least the nurse. They've got to check him over." She didn't wait for agreement or approval. She leaned down and hugged me fiercely, then rushed from the room.

Scott brushed my hair back from my forehead. He caressed my face with his fingertips. "I love you."

I rested my face against the palm of his hand. I croaked, "Love you."

"You want some water?"

I nodded. He raised the bed more upright and held the

glass for me. I took it from his hand. I found my muscles worked well enough to hold the glass and drink. The water was smooth and pleasant going down, better than chocolate syrup on a hot-fudge sundae, but not by much.

I cleared my throat several times. "I've been unconscious for two days?" My voice sounded weak and gravelly.

"Yeah, it's Monday, early evening."

"Have you called school?"

"They don't expect you back this week. Your boss and a few friends have been here."

"Not quite the way I'd like to get a week off in the middle of the year."

"Why don't you relax while I fill you in on what happened?"

I nodded. I leaned my head deeper into the pillow. With my fingertips, I caressed the hair on the back of his hand.

"There was an explosion outside the clinic. That whole block was blown to smithereens. There was a huge fire. You were pulled out of the rubble just in time. A lot of people died."

I whispered, "The last thing I remember was talking to Alvana and playing catch with her son. Are they all right?"

"We found a kid near you in the rubble. He was wearing a yellow and red outfit."

"That was Alan."

"He was alive when they rescued him. I'll try to find out how he is."

"Alvana?"

"There was a woman near the child. She was dead. I'm afraid it might have been her."

"Jesus. Alvana dead."

Alvana was the one who had asked me to come into the

clinic the first time. We had known each other since college. Back then Alvana lived in an apartment half a block from mine. She used to bake the most exquisite chocolate cakes for my birthday, and the frosting she made was unbelievably light and sweet. No one else I know has ever been able to replicate it.

It took me several minutes to digest this news. I managed to ask, "Do you know who else died?"

"I don't have a list. I didn't know that many people at the clinic, so I probably wouldn't have recognized anybody mentioned in the articles in the paper."

Scott began filling me in on the details of the scene and the rescue. When he told me about the horror while helping the victims, he began to cry. He spoke and wiped away tears at the same time. "I wasn't really scared until I got home and I could think about it. Combined with fear about you, I never expect to live through anything worse."

I pulled him close and held him. I've been in combat and know firsthand the kind of horror he was trying to get used to. I wished I could take away all those memories, his suffering, and that of the people whom he'd helped. I patted his hair, listened to his breathing, felt his muscles begin to relax. "It's going to be okay," I said.

When he finally sat back up, he said, "I think I'm supposed to be the one comforting you."

"I love you" was all I could think of to say.

After a few more minutes, he resumed his story about that night. When he got to the part about my truck, I was appalled. "You were almost killed?"

"I can hardly bear to think about it."

We'd come close to tragedy twice that night.

He quickly related the rest of the events of the past few

days. When he got to the part about the possibility of a terrorist cell across the alley, I asked, "Somebody really believes that?"

"It's the rumor. You know how that Internet crap spreads. Like butter left out to melt on a summer's day in Georgia."

I said, "Where's Pierre Salinger when we really need him?"

"We at least have Brandon Kearn."

"I'm not sure I trust him either."

"Why not?"

"I don't know. If this were a thriller novel, he'd have been dead before he got a chance to tell you what he knew."

A few minutes after Scott finished, a nurse and a doctor came in. They examined, probed, asked questions, unhooked me from a variety of machines, and declared me in acceptable and not-all-that-far-from-perfect health. They wanted to keep me overnight for further observation, but I could probably go home in the morning. The more water I sipped, the better my voice sounded.

My dad, brothers, and sister were summoned. Everybody gushed, hugged, joked, and finally left. I could have done with a few less nephews and nieces, although because it was late not a lot of the youngest ones showed up.

Finally, Scott sat at the side of the bed holding my hand. The rest had left. The hospital was quiet.

"I gotta piss," I said. "Let's see how steadily I can get to the washroom." Nobody had said I couldn't get up. Lifting my head off the pillow still caused me a little dizziness, but nothing unmanageable occurred. I swung my legs off the bed and tried to arrange my garments more modestly and comfortably. "These hospital gowns are totally useless."

"You want me to buy you some pajamas?" Scott asked.

"Just help me get to the john." I leaned on him heavily for the first few steps. My legs were a little wobbly, but I could eventually shuffle forward with a minimum of assistance.

"Why do you keep looking at the back of the hospital gown?" I asked. "I can feel a breeze."

"I like the view."

"I'm not sure this is a good time for me to be either dignified or slutty. I could use a shower and a shave." I caught my reflection in the mirror. "I must have looked worse," I muttered, "but at the moment I can't imagine when."

"You look great to me. Awake and moving."

"You could get that in a pet and not have to be in a hospital. Just think, you could listen to all the country-and-western music you want to on the stereo."

"Nobody looking at your butt would confuse you with a critter."

Scott still says things like "critter." I love him anyway. He's always liked the way my ass looks. Some people look at faces, some at crotches, some at legs, others at breasts. He's a butt man. It's okay by me.

Scott made sure I was settled on the john and left me to my privacy. I propped my elbows on my knees and held my head in my hands as I felt my body resuming expected functions. When I finished, I managed to stagger to the bathroom door on my own, but was grateful for his assistance from door to bed. I felt better for having moved. He resumed his perch on the bed. I wasn't sleepy.

I said, "I want to try calling Alvana's roommate, Patricia Rodgers. She worked in the clinic as well. She might know how other people are."

"It's late."

"I need to try. I want to know how my friends are."

"Why not save that for the morning? I'm more worried about you." Scott drew a deep breath. "I wish you didn't take so many chances."

"You take your share of them."

"But then I'm taking the chances and not you."

"And that's okay because . . . ?"

"I'm not sure. I didn't say it was rational, just that I love you, and I don't want you hurt."

Something more was bothering him, but I didn't know what. That he was upset by what had happened to me was clear. But I, who had known him for years, guessed he was holding something back. He does that at times, especially when it involves emotions. I've learned to be patient and wait for him to tell me. He's learned that it's important to recognize those things and eventually talk about them. I would wait.

I pulled him back to me and kissed him. I felt his body relax against mine. He sat back up and took more deep breaths. His eyes misted over. He wiped his hand across his face. His nickname on the team is the Iceman because he is so cool and calm in tense situations. He's always calm with even the most obnoxious reporters or interviewers. I've seen the competitive volcano under that down-on-the-farm exterior he portrays to the media. I'm one of the few people he's ever let see the intensely emotional man underneath the cool exterior. I still love the deep thrum of his voice, especially that residue of Southern drawl that sneaks in when he is deeply moved. He spoke softly, "I never want to be this scared again. I was afraid you were dead. I thought about missing you, a life without you. I don't want that to happen. I want us to have years together."

"I do too. Always. The two of us on rockers in the old gay persons' home."

He smiled. "I want them to write love songs about us, like Scarlett and Rhett."

"That wasn't a song, it was a book and a movie. She was a neurotic, conniving bitch, and he was a war profiteer. Which one do you want to be?"

"I don't think you're as dizzy or worn-out as you look. You sound pretty much like your old self."

"I'm sorry to joke. I love you. I'm sorry for the pain you've been through."

"In some ways, you're the lucky one. You've been unconscious through all this. I've been the one awake and worrying."

"I've never considered the saving graces of being in a coma. It could become the new self-help rage. Think of the ad campaign. 'We put you in a coma, not as bad as death, but better than reality.' You and I could set up our own little cult and become rich and famous. Make predictions about the end of the world. I see a whole coma cottage industry."

"Keep alliterating that way and you could be drummed out of the English teachers' union."

"I couldn't help myself. Knock me unconscious for a day or two and there's no telling what I'll alliterate."

He leaned down and gave me another quick hug.

A nurse bustled in. "Feeling better are we?"

"Very much so," I told her.

She took my temperature and blood pressure. "He should get some rest."

"I'll be going soon," Scott said. The nurse left.

I said, "I still want to try and call Alvana's roommate."

He handed me the phone, and I dialed. Patricia answered. She sounded awful. She confirmed that Alvana was dead. She also told me the names of the others from the clinic who had died. I had worked with two of them for a short time.

I said as many words of comfort as I could think of. That I was all right cheered her a bit. After I hung up, I said, "Patricia's in bad shape." I shook my head.

"You've known Alvana a long time."

I reminisced for a few minutes about the good times she and I had shared. "I'm going to miss her." My eyes misted over. A few moments later I said, "I'm going to find out who did this."

"Don't be absurd," Scott said. "How? They've got hundreds of Chicago cops working on it. What earthly good could you do? Even if the attack was directed against us, how could we possibly find out anything significant? Besides, I told you, I hired private detectives for that."

"Who did you hire?"

"Borini and Faslo."

"You didn't! They're notoriously homophobic."

"How the hell was I supposed to know that? Is there a list of required gay knowledge somewhere that you've been keeping from me? Brandon Kearn thought so too. That twit Myrtle Mae was here and said the same thing."

"Myrtle Mae showed up here?"

"And he was as snide and snotty as ever. Why do you like that creep?"

"He can be genuinely funny. I know his flair for the uselessly dramatic annoys you."

"He's developed it into a high art."

"He works very hard for many of the same causes I do. He did a lot of good work for this community for years before any of the rest of us. He was out there on his own taking risks that no one else dared to take. He lost three jobs and got beaten up numerous times before he started doing drag twenty-five years ago. Actually he's been safer in drag."

"Fine. We'll elect him saint of the millennium. I hate him.

Although he did call earlier this evening. He said a woman named Susan Clancey was planning to come to town. Myrtle Mae said you'd recognize the name."

"I know she's a doctor who performs late-term abortions. I bet he's thinking that Clancey's visit could have been connected to the clinic bombing."

"I guess so," Scott said. "Right now I don't want to talk about him or any investigation. Let's talk about what the hell we're going to do with the rest of our lives. I think we're in danger, and I think we need to take drastic action."

"Like what?"

"We need to get out of here. We should go far away. If we're really pushed to it, I can afford to buy us a small island in the South Pacific. We could be happy there."

"I'm a teacher. I have a life here. We can't just disappear off the face of the planet."

"I know you want to be independent and not beholden to my money, but we're in heaps of trouble. People are trying to kill us. You could find something to do on an island."

"I have no intention of spending my life hiding in a lead-lined bunker holding a bazooka in my hands waiting to blow to smithereens the first person to walk through the door."

"I'm talking lovely tropical island here."

"Palm trees and miles of ocean are just another kind of lead-lined bunker. Whether confined in a tight space or a hundred square miles, it means those who have threatened us have won."

"Haven't they already?"

"Running away isn't my style. Nor do I think it is a very good solution. A terrorist organization capable of the destruction they caused here would be able to buy, borrow, or steal a boat or a plane, sneak onto an island, and bomb, maim, torture, and do whatever else they enjoy doing to victims. Do an army and a navy come with the island? Or maybe it could be a 'discount island' with a limited protection warranty."

"You're the one that's hurt, and you're making jokes."

"I'm not ready to take up my machine gun and walk. At least not until tomorrow when the doctor releases me. Then I'll be ready."

"You want us to just parade ourselves around the countryside?" Scott asked.

"Which we've done a lot of. We both willingly went on all those talk shows. I don't regret that decision. I'm going to be part of finding out what the hell is going on. Whether or not the threats against us are mixed up in the bombing, I'm going to work on it. This is going to stop."

"How?"

"You already said my school doesn't expect me back this week. I'm going to spend the time figuring things out."

"I wish you wouldn't."

"You want to help?"

"I'm not feeling like I have a lot of choices here. If I let you go by yourself, I'll feel guilt about not helping. I'd be worried every minute you're gone."

"Here I am awake only a few hours and inflicting guilt on the one I love the best. I must be close to one hundred percent better."

"Joke if you like. I'm really worried."

We sat in silence for a few moments. Finally, I said, "I'm sorry about my levity. Maybe it's just nervous relief." I shifted in the bed. My butt was sore. "We both know we probably can do little, if anything, to help solve the major crime here. By doing something proactive, I think we can at least give ourselves some peace of mind about the personal threats."

"Do you think you can stop them?"

"The more we can find out the better."

We looked at each other brown eyes to blue. I'm a sucker for that puppy-dog look of his. Have been since the day I met him. It also turns me on. So, I'm afraid at that moment, memories of him naked mingled with less pornographic love and affection.

At last he nodded slightly. "Okay, I'll help. What do we do first?"

"We could start with that typed note that was found here. We should be able to get a list of who's working on this floor. Would a criminal be fortunate enough to have a job in the exact spot I happen to be brought to? Unlikely. It was probably somebody from outside, but we'll keep the list handy for cross-reference. We can check if Borini and Faslo found anything out. Although if they're homophobic, maybe they won't do all that much."

"I offered them an awful lot of money, and they turned it down. That's got to be a positive sign."

"I hope so. I also think we should work on the explosion."

"I thought you said it wouldn't do any good to investigate that."

"No, I don't think we'll be able to solve it," I said, "but I think we can nose around the edges and with any luck find out something that relates to our problem."

"That doesn't sound plausible."

"It's more plausible than running to an island or trying to hide in a lead-lined bunker."

"You're the one who mentioned the lead-lined bunker," Scott pointed out.

"No bunker, no island. We find out what we can about the threats and the explosion. If the two meet in the middle, I'd be stunned, but I want to try both. I know we can't interview every suspect, but we do have connections."

Scott nodded and touched my hand. "If you promise to be very careful, and keep guards around and not take any risks."

"What about your guards and Kearn's news about McCutcheon?"

"I still trust him," Scott said.

"I don't think we can trust anybody at this point."

After a few moments, he said, "Look, we are not alone against the world. We have friends. We have people who care about us. We can't do this by ourselves. We've got to trust someone at some point."

"For now I'm suggesting a healthy skepticism about everybody until we find out incontrovertibly that they can be trusted."

"I suppose we really don't have much choice."

"I agree." I sat up a little straighter in the bed. "The first thing we need to do is find out the name and background of every fatality and those who survived, what they did before, who they're related to, everything."

"How do you plan to get that?"

"That guy Pulver from the Chicago police seems like a good possibility."

"I'll talk to McCutcheon about setting up an appointment."

"Please do. We'll start there in the morning."

The nurse entered again. She insisted that I get some sleep. Although I was keyed up to take some action in our defense, once Scott had left and the lights were turned off, I felt myself getting drowsy. As I drifted off, I recalled the image of the guard standing outside my door.

ˎ14ˏ

The next morning I only felt a trifle woozy. I got to the bathroom myself. The shave and shower felt great. Getting out of the hospital gown and dressed in the clothes Scott had brought felt terrific. Eating a decent meal felt even better. I think hospital food is okay. I figure if I don't have to cook it or clean up afterward, it's gourmet.

Then I got annoyed waiting for the appropriate hospital personnel to show up so I could officially leave. While waiting, I tracked down Alan Redpath. He was in the same hospital, in pediatric intensive care. They didn't know if he would survive. I managed to look in on him. He seemed to be hooked up to far more machines than I had been. Watching the poor kid sleep made me more determined than ever to find out who had blown up the clinic.

Scott arrived before nine. He looked as if he'd been through the explosion. I hugged him. "You look awful," I said.

"If I get to sleep, I start to have nightmares about the victims I helped."

"You were almost one yourself."

"I know. That scares me a little too."

I tried to reassure him. "It's going to take time. It's not easy to get used to what you saw."

"I wish it would be sooner rather than later. I just want to be at peace." I told him about Alan Redpath.

"Poor kid," Scott said.

The doctor showed up, spent less than five minutes, and told me I could go.

Once in the car, I said, "I want to go to the bomb site."

"Why?"

"I want to look." McCutcheon was with us. He raised no objections. I really didn't want to talk with the guard around. I wasn't about to ask him for permission to do anything, either.

On the way over, McCutcheon said, "I've made a few more calls on Borini and Faslo, like I promised. I heard nothing suspicious and couldn't find anyone ready to bad-mouth them. As for that employee's gay discrimination suit, the guy was supposed to be an incompetent dolt who got himself fired for being unable to run some software he claimed he'd had training in. He's been fired from four other jobs. Three before and one after."

We parked the car as near as possible to the site and strolled over. The temperature was above normal. The smell of damp and burning permeated the air. Crowds still gathered at the periphery of the scene. To keep from being recognized, we wore baseball caps pulled down over our eyes and cheap sunglasses. Many times this simple ensemble keeps the curious from recognizing us.

Among the onlookers, I saw Mrs. Fattatuchi clutching the arm of her oldest daughter. Periodically, I saw her raise a tissue to her eyes. She seemed to be just staring. I didn't know her personally, so I didn't feel comfortable going up to her to talk.

After we'd made a complete circuit of the site, we stood at the viewpoint closest to the rear of what had been the clinic. Puddles of water reflected the scattered clouds. The aboveground remnants of the buildings were charred by fire. The air reeked of smoke and burned flesh. We could see rescue workers hunting for survivors and the dead in the unburned remnants of the health club across the street.

The police crime-scene tape kept us more than a block away, but from the various vantage points we gaped from, I could still see how massive the destruction had been. Seeing the reality of what had happened made the extent of my good fortune stunningly clear. Part of my survival had been due to solid masonry and concrete abutments used by the builders of a century ago. Perhaps my survival was also due to my tiny and cramped work space and that a little boy had dropped a ball. It had always seemed so confining and uncomfortable, designed more for hiding than working.

I was staggered at the enormity of not being among the dead amid so much destruction. Several unremoved burned-out cars reminded me of how close Scott had come to being immolated. That thought smote me most intensely at that moment.

Every once in a while I ruminate about the decisions I've made in my life. The moments of change, the moments when everything would have been different if I'd made another choice. There were lots of regrets and satisfactions mixed with big and little decisions. In retrospect, joining the marines had been a huge mistake. Some of the fortunate turnings had been blind luck. Hindsight said being in a monogamous relationship since before the AIDS epidemic had been fortuitous indeed. I'd had my share of hot one-night

117

stands, but before the plague. Luck and random chance rather than choice as ruling elements in my life were not an attractive thought. I like to believe that I am in control of my fate. I don't like to face the fact that I'm not. Deep down I can't imagine that there is some grand scheme for why things happen. I look at a universe consisting mostly of unimaginable vastnesses of indifference, and I can only see that we are born, live, and die more by random chance than most of us care to admit. Belief is nice as a concept and is reassuring to a lot of people. It just isn't enough for me.

At the moment I felt overwhelmed by what I saw and felt. I became dizzy and staggered slightly. I leaned heavily on Scott's arm.

"You okay?" he asked.

"I'm not sure I can do this."

"Do what?"

"Be as brave and active as I said in the hospital." I pointed at the scene in front of us. "This is too much."

"You were in combat."

"It's not the same. That was far away and foreign. This is at home, where I live. There you live by chance and chaos is expected. I was young and stupid. It was easy to be oblivious at a moment's notice. Here the world is supposed to be ordered. That was many years ago. This is too overwhelming."

"You already knew it was bigger than us. I know you. You're going to get involved. This is personal. Someone you know died in the explosion. You don't give up that easy. If you didn't work on it, you'd be miserable."

Brandon Kearn emerged from behind a slew of television trucks from CNN, WGN, WBBM, WLS, WMAQ, CLTV, WFLD, and MCT.

"Good to see you out of the hospital," he said to me.

"Thanks for coming to see me," I replied. Scott had told

me about Kearn's visits. "You're still reporting from the scene?"

"Mostly getting some background shots for the continuing coverage. It would be great to do an interview with you guys. It would give me something to lead the news with."

"Not right now," I said.

"If the rest of the crews over there get a whiff that you're here, you won't have much choice."

"We should move off," Scott said.

"I wanted to talk to you anyway," Kearn said. We strolled southward. At the next corner he drew us aside so McCutcheon could not hear. "My fire department contact called me again. He really wants to talk to you guys."

"Good," I said.

He gave us a slip of paper. "He's expecting a call."

"What does the fire department guy know?" Scott asked.

"Details."

"You can't just tell us?" Scott asked.

I said, "I'd like to get the information firsthand."

"Your buddy is right," Kearn said. "If you're going to ask questions, it's better to get the information directly from the source. Good reporters know that. You don't want someone interpreting for you. Plus, if you're suspicious of everyone, as I think you should be, then you shouldn't trust me either."

"Why would he talk to us?" Scott asked.

"He's gay and he's sympathetic to your cause."

"The international gay conspiracy strikes again," I said.

"I wish I had one of those," Kearn said. "Hell of a lot easier to get information. Have you heard they found William Portmeister in the rubble of the health club?"

"Who's he?" I asked.

"He owns MCT. Near him they found Alderman Allen. They'd been reported missing but weren't found until early

119

this morning. The two of them worked out every Saturday evening, then took their wives out to dinner, very clubby and fashionable. Two other executives from the network were there, but they were in a different part of the building. They survived."

"Did you know any of them personally?"

"I'd met Portmeister once or twice. I didn't know the others. The death count is over fifty now."

I asked, "With a dead alderman, is this going to turn into something political?"

"A dead Chicago alderman?" Kearn said. "Why would someone go to all this trouble for one of them? If you wait just a little while, he'd probably be indicted for something and thrown in jail."

"Any reason to think the health club was the target?"

"Not that I know of. It was directly across the alley from where the truck was placed. You figure if it was the target, they would have parked it closer."

I asked, "Do you have a list of who died?"

Kearn pulled out a dog-eared piece of paper and handed it to me. "I haven't had time to check many of these people out. We're starting to get data released to the media on some of the victims. A lot of this is going to start appearing in the paper. I know the three women at the top of the list were in the clinic. All were pregnant. They were in a waiting room. They're all dead."

I shook my head. I was still leaning on Scott. Seeing this scroll of the dead renewed my feeling of vulnerability. I looked for Susan Clancey's name. It wasn't there.

"Do you know who Susan Clancey is?" I asked him.

"A woman who performs late-term abortions. What about her?"

"We heard a rumor that she was supposed to be in town on Saturday."

"I haven't heard a word. Nothing has been on the wires about her. Thanks for the tip." Kearn pointed at the paper he'd given me. "I should have these lists earlier than most people. Call me periodically, and I'll update you. I gave Scott my pager number."

Scott asked, "Have you managed to get an interview with that Lyle Gibson, the head of the clinic protesters?"

"I'm still working on it. He's usually eager to get as much publicity as possible."

Kearn pulled us slightly farther down the street away from McCutcheon. As he handed us another slip of paper, he lowered his voice. "This is the name of the reporter who knew McCutcheon in Bosnia. You need to call him. I get uneasy every time I see you guys with him. You better check this out first."

Scott looked hesitant. I took the paper and nodded. I asked, "Would it be possible to view the videotape that you got that night? I want to see everything I can about what happened. Looking at the video will give me more of a sense of reality. In some ways I feel disconnected, because I didn't actually experience what happened. I've seen the aftermath. Maybe the tape will give me a clue. I might recognize someone or something out of place."

"Sure, I can arrange it."

I said, "You know, I appreciate all your help, but I've been wanting to ask something." Kearn nodded. "One thing I don't get from what Scott told me is you deciding to investigate. Are your bosses urging you to? How can you expect to succeed when all these police officers are working on the case?"

"It isn't a question of absolutely succeeding. It's more I've been permanently assigned to the story and given time and staff to develop any lead I can. Sure, I'd like to find the killer. I think I'm more likely to advance my career because of this explosion. I hope my being blatant about my ambition doesn't annoy you. My goal for now is to insinuate myself into any parts of this investigation that I can. If I get leads, I follow them. If I get cops to talk to me, I'm lucky. I'm not going to be like most of these drones sitting at press conferences called by spokespeople for the police where reporters ask repetitious and silly questions."

Scott said, "Sunday morning you sounded ready to quit being a reporter."

"I still might. If I can, I want to put a human face to this tragedy—real stories about real people. At the same time, if I stay in this career, this is the biggest thing I may ever cover. I don't have any illusion that I'll solve the case, but I do recognize the fact that we make our own luck. I'm just as likely to find out who did it as you are."

Scott asked, "You aren't worried it might be dangerous if you actually did find the killer?"

"Maybe I'm too confident or too naive or too ambitious. I'll try to avoid hubris, but not to the exclusion of getting the story."

Scott said, "Maybe you'd feel different if you'd been personally threatened like we have."

"Do you have proof the bombing is connected to the threats against you?"

"No," Scott said.

"If you get any, please let me know."

"Why are you willing to help us?" I asked.

"I told your lover, random chance could break in my favor. I've got you talking to me. I'll take any lead and any chance. Plus, Scott still has some value as a person to be interviewed as one of the rescuers. He's famous so he's part of the story."

I said, "Like you, we're going to do whatever little bit makes sense. You think you're using us, but we're using you as well. I suspect we'll get more from you than the reverse."

"If we're lucky, it will be mutual," Kearn said. "I don't think you should get your hopes up."

I said, "My hopes aren't up. I realize the impossibility of what I want to do, but if I don't try, then I'll never know what I could have accomplished."

Kearn wished us luck and reminded us to keep in touch. As we turned to go, McCutcheon shouted at us. He rushed forward and shoved Scott and me aside. Kearn jumped into the street. A black Mercedes with tinted windows ran halfway up onto the curb. It missed Scott's left foot by a yard, and Kearn's bent-over form by only a few inches. The car crushed a no-parking sign, of which there are all too many on the near west and north sides of Chicago. I never saw the brake lights flash on as the Mercedes rushed away from us.

We got up and dusted ourselves off. It had happened too fast for any of us to get the license number of the car.

Scott asked, "Was that aimed at us or simply an accident?"

Kearn asked, "And which of us was it aimed at?"

I said, "Hard to tell. Whoever it is has enough money to afford an expensive car."

"And tinted windows," Scott added.

"Which are illegal in Chicago," McCutcheon said.

"They are?" Scott asked.

"Yep," McCutcheon said.

Kearn asked, "Do you have any specific idea of who would be after you?"

"We don't have a clue at the moment," I said. "Staring at

where the car disappeared won't get us anywhere." They turned to look at me. "We've got a lot of work left to do. Thanks for your help so far. You've helped us, we'll try to help you. We'll talk again."

We agreed to that and parted.

"Another in a long string of coincidences?" I asked the two of them.

"I think so," McCutcheon said.

I thought he spoke much too quickly and much too confidently.

⌐ 15 ⌐

We used Scott's cell phone to call Angus Thieme, Kearn's
reporter contact. He wasn't in his hotel room. We called his
news affiliate in Chicago. Scott used his name and fame to
get through the layers of secretaries and flunkies. I told Scott
to set up the meeting in Thieme's hotel room.

"Why his hotel room?" Scott asked after he hung up.

"We're investigating our guard. We can leave him downstairs in the hotel and go up to the room ourselves, and if
necessary, we can ditch him afterward."

Scott said, "I think the argument still applies. If he's one
of the people trying to kill you, me, or both of us, he's had
plenty of chances. If he's keeping track of us for some obscure reason, another hour or so of him hanging around can't
make that much difference. If he's innocent, we haven't lost
anything."

McCutcheon drove us to the Marriott on Michigan Avenue. McCutcheon made no demur as we left him in the lobby
and proceeded up to the twentieth floor.

Angus Thieme was a bear of a man in his late fifties or early sixties. He was over six feet tall with a snowy white beard that connected to the fringe of hair encircling his bald head. He wore a khaki jacket over khaki pants and a blue shirt. He offered us bourbon and we declined, but he took half a glassful.

He grinned at us as we sat down. "I don't usually get these high-class rooms. I'm used to being on the road in very unpleasant hovels. I've slept outdoors more than I care to admit. I can always tell a hotel that thinks it's high-class. You get an iron and an ironing board in your room. First thing I always think of when I show up in town, what is it that I have to iron?" Abruptly, he changed topics. "You've made a lot of news this year. How are you both doing?"

"It's been like a circus," Scott said.

"News reporting can be like that," Thieme said, "but you seem to have handled it well."

"As good as we could," I said.

Thieme said, "Sensible answer."

I said, "Brandon Kearn told us you had some information for us. We're not sure if we can trust him."

He shrugged. "As much as any reporter. I've heard of him, which is a little odd for someone not on a national network, although Chicago is a pretty big market. He's very ambitious and out for himself, but he's been extremely helpful on several projects I was working on. The kid has great instincts. If he isn't blinded by the cameras, he could become a good reporter someday. Still, I'd love to shave that cemented hair completely off. I have a suspicion that his relentless ambition is a cover for a soft interior. I like him, and he asked me to help you out."

I said, "We appreciate anything you can tell us."

"You've heard the rumor about the secret terrorist cell,

Tools of Satan, being the target and not the clinic?"

"Is anybody taking that seriously?" I asked.

"It's hard to discount anything in a catastrophe of this magnitude and complexity."

"It's from the Internet," I said. "Who believes anything on there?"

"No one with a modicum of sense, but the idea won't go away. It keeps picking up steam. I've been running around for hours trying to find a shred of evidence. Haven't gotten any yet."

I asked, "What do you know about Ken McCutcheon?"

Thieme said, "I've got five people to interview this afternoon so I'll make this quick. You might think of ditching your guard."

"You need to tell us why," Scott said.

"I knew him in Bosnia five years ago. He was practically just a kid. He was not using the name McCutcheon. Yesterday, I saw him in the background in one of the stories about your truck being blown up. Rumors in Bosnia said he was connected with the militia movements here."

"What proof do you have for that?" Scott asked.

"Enough for me. Not enough for a jury. I assumed he was still hiring himself out around the world someplace. I hear there's a big market in Russia for skulking, sneaking, and assassinating. To be sure of my memory and my observation, I tried to contact some folks I knew in Bosnia. He was using the name Forandi in Bosnia. This guy can be extremely dangerous. How did you come to hire him?"

Scott explained.

"And that's it?" Thieme said. "You believed that?"

"They're good friends. They trusted him. He's been fantastic. I've had zero trouble since I hired him."

"He couldn't stop the phone calls," I said.

Thieme said, "I know somebody who's a specialist in militia groups. The cops don't like to admit it, but they've asked him to come to town. He's the best. He's a friend of mine. He'll be able to give you more information. I'll talk to him for you so he'll expect your call."

Scott asked, "Would McCutcheon have the nerve to set himself up in a legitimate business if he was a member of one of these groups? Someone would eventually find out, wouldn't they?"

"Don't militia group people have real jobs?" Thieme asked, and then answered his own question. "Of course they do. Somebody's got to pay the bills."

I said, "I thought they just lived off the land and wrote bad checks."

Scott said, "You're saying he might be a danger?"

"I'm reasonably certain this is the right guy. I only saw him for a few seconds on one report. I haven't heard of any gay-supportive militia groups so I think he'd be a danger to you. Gay people are generally on their dislike lists. None of this, however, is my main story, yet. It's something I'm keeping in mind. I've got other leads to track first."

I asked, "Could we talk to your Bosnia sources?"

"A young reporter who now lives in this country made a pass at Forandi/McCutcheon in Bosnia. He beat the hell out of the reporter. Homophobia sucks." Thieme wrote down a name and number and handed it to me. The name Toby Ratshinski meant nothing to me. The area code was 212, New York.

"Use my name," Thieme said. "He'll talk to you." He also gave us the name of his expert on militia groups and the hotel where he was staying.

"What if McCutcheon isn't the guy you think he is?"

"Can you guys afford to take that chance?"

128

"He's waiting for us downstairs. Would you come take a look?"

"I can take a discreet glance."

On the way down in the elevator I asked, "Have you ever heard of Susan Clancey, a woman who performs late-term abortions? She was supposedly coming to town."

"I never heard of her, but that isn't odd. I mostly do stories with international connections if I'm not actually overseas covering something. I'm in this country less than a full month a year."

I asked, "What do you do in an investigation like this?"

"Try to sort through the bull slung around at the official press conferences. Try to develop my own contacts. Try to do a little poking around on my own. Try to do a lot of basic legwork. A lot of modern reporting is telling the camera the obvious. Mostly I'll give updates to the network that there has been no progress. After a week or so I move on to the next international crisis. Are you saying this Dr. Clancey is someone I should be investigating?"

"I don't know," I said. "Lots of violence has happened when she's gone to other towns."

On the ground floor, McCutcheon noticed us, but didn't come over. Thieme chatted with us about the weather as he surreptitiously examined McCutcheon. At last, he shook his head. "I think it's him. In Bosnia the guy I'm talking about had dyed-black hair."

Scott said, "I find it hard to believe he was disguising himself with just a dye job."

"Why disguise himself at all?" I asked.

Thieme shrugged. "I don't know. I'm just giving information. His hair was dyed that odd way they do now. Just the stuff on the top of the head. I've never understood that. It's a trend started by people I never want to have to interview."

"But it might not be him?" I asked.

"Sorry. You'll need to talk to my source. This guy could be the brother of the guy I'm thinking of or not him at all. Put me on a witness stand and I couldn't be sure. In my opinion, it probably is him."

▄ 16 ▄

Thieme left.

Scott asked, "Do I fire McCutcheon?"

"Yes," I replied immediately.

"You're getting ahead of any facts that we have. Remember, he hasn't proved a danger to us yet. And what do we do for protection if I do fire him?"

"There's other firms. If he's who Thieme says he is, he's a danger to us."

"He was walking with me to your truck the other night. He could have been killed. If he's a danger, I don't see him connected to the people trying to attack us. I'm going to go with my gut feeling. Whatever McCutcheon's story is, he's been faithful to me. Why would he be, if he's out to do me or you harm?"

"I don't know."

"Until we get specific knowledge, I'm sticking with him."

I had no plausible arguments to refute Scott's logic. We used the pay phone in the lobby to try to call Thieme's contact in New York. We got an answering machine. I decided not to leave a message.

"You know," I said before we strolled over to McCutcheon, "if he's out to get us, having him around means he knows our every move."

Scott put his hand on my arm to stop me. "I'm kind of tired of this semi-cloak-and-dagger crap. I know you're just out of the hospital, but this is getting to be a bit much. You don't like him. That is not criminal. I remember your reasons for disapproving of him. 'He's too pretty to have his own agency.' That logic sucks a hell of a lot more than the reasons I used to hire him."

"That was more a joke than anything."

"I wasn't laughing. Your comments were dismissive and condescending. You don't make shallow judgments based on looks. That's not the kind of person you are. Why'd you do it this time?"

I hate it when he's insightful, reasonable, and right. "I admit I was too flip, but you were too hasty."

"Maybe" was all the admission he gave.

"My gut feeling says he's a rat. Your gut feeling says he's okay. I hope you're right. I'll agree to a truce about him until we know more. Okay?"

Scott agreed.

We stood across the lobby from McCutcheon. He nodded at us. "What now?" Scott asked.

"We could try Pulver," I said.

We called, but he couldn't meet us for several hours.

Next, we called Jack Wolf, Kearn's contact in the fire department. He agreed to meet us at Ann Sather's restaurant on Belmont.

When we arrived, we asked for a seat in the farthest room from the sidewalk. We huddled in a corner hidden from most observers in the restaurant. We asked McCutcheon to sit farther up front. Every few moments Scott peeked around the corner to see if Wolf had arrived.

In the meantime the waitress plunked a plate of confections on our table. These included the famed cinnamon rolls.

I began to wonder if McCutcheon himself wasn't a magnet. Maybe he wasn't a specific danger, but if someone was single-minded enough to follow us around, then maybe they were able to recognize and remember our guards. Being a crazed killer didn't inherently imply stupidity, although it probably helps.

Scott recognized Wolf when he walked in and waved him over. Wolf sat down and ordered coffee. "You guys doing better?" His voice was a soft rumble.

I shrugged. "The doctor says I'm fine."

He turned to Scott. "You?"

"I'm having trouble sleeping at night."

"You look like hell."

The coffee arrived. Wolf grasped his with two large hands and took a deep gulp. He grabbed a roll and took a huge bite.

Scott asked, "How do you get over the horrors that you see?"

Wolf chewed, swallowed, sipped coffee, and then said, "At first, you never think you will. Then later you wonder how you ever became immune. If you think about the process of going from terror to insensitivity, or if you dwell on the fact that there will always be another horror, then you quit and get out. You realize if you didn't become immune, you'd probably go crazy. If you stay, you remember that you're saving lives, that you're a respected member of the community, that your job can make a real difference to real people in dramatic, concrete ways. Give it time." He gulped more coffee.

I said, "You wanted to see us."

"Yep."

"Why?"

He pointed at Scott. "I saw you that night working at the site. I also saw you in the news coverage." Wolf nodded at me. "I heard you were hurt in the explosion. Kearn told me you were trying to find out who was making threats against you, and maybe trying to find out who did the bombing."

"Do you think the two are connected?" I asked.

"I don't think so. The bomber was most likely making a political statement. Maybe he or she is a very nasty killer covering their tracks, but would they need this much destruction to get at one person? And if it was to get at one person, there is no proof that one person is you."

I said, "For a murderer it would also be an almost sure way of never getting caught. Who would suspect a nonterrorist group?"

"Mostly we're investigating the threats against us," Scott said. "I've also hired Borini and Faslo."

"Aren't they notoriously homophobic?" Wolf asked.

"Nobody ever mentioned it to me," Scott said.

"Haven't there been articles about them in the local papers?" Wolf asked. "I read about them being sued for firing somebody because they were gay."

"I'm out of town a lot," Scott said. "I must've missed it."

"It was several summers ago," I said. "You might have been on the road with the team."

Wolf added, "It didn't make big headlines."

"You're gay?" I asked.

"That's one of the reasons I want to help. I admire what Scott has done. I'm willing to do what I can to help you guys out."

"What do you know?" I asked.

"It was definitely a fuel-oil-and-fertilizer bomb like the one

134

in Oklahoma City. It was in a semitrailer truck. Fortunately, a lot of the force blew out of the back of the truck. There's still a crater, but the main force blew itself out both sides of the alley."

"I was working near the alley but at the other end of the block and in the basement."

"You were lucky."

"I know." I shuddered. "Have they found enough pieces of the truck to be able to get any hard data about it?"

"I'm on the investigating team helping to find stuff in the debris. What we've found has been fairly ordinary so far."

"Then why are we here?" I asked.

"A couple of gay guys on the department were talking. We get together once a week to talk and play some poker. We're not a club or anything, and we don't meet in public. It's very discreet. We aren't political. A couple of them heard some of the investigators talking about you guys at the site."

"What'd they say?"

"That the 'faggots being involved' made this complicated. The Chicago cops that they overheard were planning to do background checks on you guys to see if there was anything suspicious about you."

I said, "And we just happened to park our explosive-filled truck in this alley, and we accidentally almost killed one of us?"

"This wouldn't be the first time the bombers killed one of their own."

"Sounds far-fetched," I said.

"Homophobia can make people pretty blind," Wolf said.

This obscure warning was all he knew. I began to suspect he'd traded his bit of knowledge for a chance to do some celebrity jock-sniffing.

Afterward, outside the restaurant, Scott said, "He didn't know shit."

I said, "It's time to see Pulver." The tac-team officer had agreed to meet with us in a coffee shop on Milwaukee Avenue just north of Belmont. "We've also got to resolve the McCutcheon issue. I think we should fire him. It might even be safer not having anything to do with Pulver."

"And then we get no inside information and no protection," Scott said.

"Unless the two of them are in on something together."

"I think you're starting to go off the deep end with this paranoia."

"Going off the deep end is one of the important charms of being paranoid."

Scott frowned.

I continued, "Let's just tell McCutcheon the problem. Why make it a big secret? What do we have to hide from him?"

"You can't just tell your security guard you think he might be in a conspiracy against you."

"Sure I can. Why not? What do we lose?"

Scott began another protest, but my mind was made up. I felt no need to hide my suspicions. Nor was I going to start lying to save McCutcheon's feelings or his job as Scott's security guard. I walked over to McCutcheon. "We've been warned that you might be homophobic and a danger to us. I can't think of a way to get rid of you, and Scott won't fire you. We want to talk to Pulver without you, but we're not sure how to do that. Scott still wants you as security guard."

"Who told you to be suspicious of me?"

Avoiding a direct answer, I said, "We heard you beat up a gay guy who came on to you in Bosnia."

"Which version of that story did you get?"

"I beg your pardon?"

"There are generally three versions. The heart of all of them is I beat somebody up. One, after I let an army sergeant screw me, I beat him up in a psychotic homophobic reaction. Another, I let a reporter screw me and crushed his skull for the same reason I smashed the sergeant. The third, that I tried to give a blow job to a reporter and he threatened to out me, and I killed him to stop him."

I said, "So many stories must mean there's plausibility involved somewhere."

"I doubt if the truth would convince you."

"We've been given a number of someone to call."

"Call them."

"What is the real story?" Scott asked.

McCutcheon said, "I won't work at cross-purposes with you. Obviously, someone has convinced you that I'm a threat. I still want to help you be safe. If you're going to continue investigating, you're going to be in more danger, not less." His handsome face was creased in a worried frown. "I told Clay that I would vouch for both of you. I'll make sure he will continue to talk to you and give you information."

Scott said, "I don't think you're a threat."

"I do," I added immediately.

McCutcheon said, "No matter. You need to feel safe. I don't make you feel that way. I don't see a point in forcing you to change that opinion. I'm going to bow out of your lives. At the same time, you should have some kind of protection. I can recommend another firm, or if you don't trust me to do that, you can check any other contacts you may have. If you want, I'll hang around until you can find someone else. Or if you want me to walk out right now, I will. It is up to you guys." He looked from one to the other of us.

Scott said, "Give us a minute, would you?"

We moved up the street in front of a currency exchange.

Scott said, "We're in over our heads on this one. We're disagreeing over something pretty fundamental. I don't want to fight over this. I'm afraid our disagreement is going to get in the way of what is best for us."

Scott's calm and reasonableness in a crisis could drive a saint nuts. It's also one of the many reasons I love him.

He continued, "You're only hours out of a hospital. I think we need to step back for a minute and think. We're both emotionally vulnerable because of what we've been through. You're angry about what happened to yourself and to your friend. That certainly justifies self-righteous anger. Does it justify spewing it out at every turn? Maybe you'll direct it at someone disposed to be on our side, and they'll be turned off instead of motivated to help."

I couldn't deny the sensibleness of his reasoning. "I don't want to give up trying to find things out."

"Okay, but can we pause right now, just for a minute? There's no immediate danger this second. We need to think and plan."

I drew a deep breath and leaned back against the building.

Scott said, "First of all, I'd say McCutcheon's reaction is pretty much exactly what I would like someone I trust to say at a moment like this."

"Yeah, it was."

"I want to keep him. There isn't going to be a way to be sure we can trust him until we do a lot more checking. Remember, I tried to do that when we hired him."

"We've got that contact from Angus Thieme," I said. "This goes beyond the mystery-man image McCutcheon tries to portray. Everybody's got secrets, but usually a time comes when it's important or necessary to tell."

"We can work on discovering the truth. Until we find out more, I think we should keep him on. He's had innumerable chances to do us genuine harm. Why he would have waited this long to act is unfathomable to me. Isn't it unreasonable to just dismiss him?"

"What's happened to me is beyond unreasonable, but I guess you're right. For now, I'm willing to go with your instinct. At the least, though, he should wait outside while we do all our interviews."

"Okay."

We walked back to McCutcheon and told him what we had decided. He nodded. "That'll be fine until you get a new security firm."

"We're not asking you to quit," Scott said.

McCutcheon said, "As soon as this mess is resolved, I think it would be best."

Scott looked annoyed, but kept quiet. We left it at that.

17

The coffee shop was in a neighborhood changing from rundown ethnic to rehabbed overpriced. The vinyl on the booths was ripped, the floor had specks of dust probably there since the Depression, and the walls had pictures that Norman Rockwell would have thought were too treacly.

As we walked in, Scott pointed to a man in a back booth and said, "That's him."

Pulver waved us over.

Pulver wore sunglasses, a brown and white western shirt, black jeans, and black cowboy boots. He looked like a lean cowboy ready to go out and rope a few steers or punch a few cows. He wasn't handsome, but whippet thin, a panther down on the range. He could be a poster boy for what rugged and tough should look like.

Pulver smiled at us as Scott did the introductions. "You feeling better?" Pulver asked. The accent was South Side of Chicago, but soft and deep. You could almost picture a cowboy around the campfire murmuring to his buddies after a long day in the saddle. He gave meaning to the concept I've heard some gay men express that if there were reincarnation, they'd like to come back as a cowboy's saddle.

I said, "Just about a hundred percent." Actually, I still felt a bit light-headed. Scott looked as if he could use several nights' sleep.

Scott and I ordered soft drinks. Pulver asked for tea. McCutcheon said, "Clay, I'm going to sit at the counter, but I want you to give them as much information as you can."

"What's up?" Pulver asked.

"We're having paranoia problems," I said.

McCutcheon said, "It's important, Clay. They can explain it as well as I can. They need you." McCutcheon walked away.

Pulver shook his head. "Kenny really likes you both. I trust him and I owe him. Although, when I'm done with you guys, I'll have paid him back twice over. It'll be nice to have him owe me for a change."

I said, "I'm working from the assumption that we shouldn't trust anyone. Until we get some definitive answers, we trust nobody, including you and McCutcheon."

"Why would I give you information if I'm out to get you?"

"I don't think Tom's being logical," Scott said.

"Someone told us to be suspicious of McCutcheon. You came to us through him. Therefore, I'm suspicious of you."

Pulver frowned. "I'm not the one who was in the middle of a bombing, nor am I the one who keeps getting threats, so I've got a lot of sympathy for your fear. But if you don't trust me, why would you be trusting what I have to say to you?"

"Exactly," Scott said.

That logic had me stumped. I went back to my question. "What's the deal between you and McCutcheon? Are you lovers?"

Pulver rubbed his chin the way the aged, grizzled prospector always does in old movie westerns. "I'd rather you trusted me. I'm willing to go a little way to earn your trust because I think you need help."

"I'm sorry I'm being so paranoid," I said. "I just figure it's best to be cautious."

Pulver nodded. "I was born and raised on the far southwest side of Chicago. I am not as prejudiced and bigoted as most people think that makes me. Kenny and I went through kindergarten to tenth grade together. Kenny and me are tied to the old neighborhood and to each other, but we are not and have never been lovers. As far as I know, he doesn't have anyone special now."

"We heard that he punched a guy in Bosnia after he had sex with him."

"Lots of crazy rumors can start for any number of reasons. Do you guys think he's a threat to you?"

"Yes," I said.

"Stop," Scott ordered. "I for one appreciate Pulver's and McCutcheon's help and patience." Scott placed his hand on my arm. "We can play the 'who's more paranoid' version of 'who do you trust' and 'who's a threat' until we all bore each other to tears. Let's get on with it." He looked at Pulver. "You tell us stuff. We find out over time if it's believable or not. If the information you give us is false and gets us killed, we won't be able to come back and say I told you so. With luck we'll come out alive and with a solution at the end."

"Eminently sensible," Pulver said.

I kept my mouth shut. I was beginning to feel a bit foolish. I could never be a right-wing preacher. Self-righteous posturing, as I'd been doing, gets old very quickly. I realized my unreasonableness was approaching the level of irrationality. I decided to give it a rest. I just had to hope backing off didn't get us killed.

"You still aren't part of the team working on the investigation?" Scott asked.

"No. The rest of the criminals of Chicago have not used the explosion as an excuse to call a moratorium on their criminal activities. In fact my partner and I helped bust a small heroin operation last night."

"What can you tell us about the bombing?" Scott asked.

"Couple things. You know the Fattatuchis, the owner of the deli that was destroyed?"

We nodded.

"Their son is a member of a right-wing militia group. He dined in their restaurant earlier that evening. We're looking for him, but haven't been able to contact him."

"He'd be hard to miss," I said. "He's always dressed in leather and tries to look like a terrorist."

Scott said, "Myrtle Mae talked about a guy in leather he had his eye on in the restaurant. He said it was their son." Scott gave us the description.

"Sounds like him," I said.

"Who is Myrtle Mae?" Pulver asked.

I explained.

"I'll have to make sure he's on the list of people the police have to talk to."

"He doesn't know anything," Scott said.

"He was there," Pulver said. "That's enough to get him at least a simple visit."

"If we're lucky, he'll get locked up for a crime," Scott said.

"We heard that Susan Clancey was supposed to be in town."

"Who's she?" Pulver asked.

I said, "A woman who performs late-term abortions around the country. Quite often major demonstrations occur when she comes to a town to do the procedure."

"I haven't heard anything about her."

"She tries to keep a very low profile wherever she goes."

"You're saying she could have been a focal point? Where'd you get this information?"

Scott said, "From that Myrtle Mae we told you about."

"How would he know that?"

I said, "I'm not sure. He does seem to know a lot of people and often has inside information."

"We'll have to find out what he knows."

"The Fattatuchis' son really is a terrorist?" Scott asked.

"Would he really blow up his own family's restaurant?" I asked.

"I find that hard to believe," Scott said.

Pulver said, "We know he's a member of a group, but we don't know anything beyond that. He may have an alibi. He may simply march around in the woods on weekends, a glorified Boy Scout with a lethal weapon. Despite the headlines about those groups, most of them are still pretty small, filled with loons working scams not to pay their taxes."

I asked, "What else can you tell us about the bombing?"

"The offices of Freedom's Children were in the building that was completely destroyed directly north across the alley from the clinic."

"Who are Freedom's Children?"

"A right-to-life group."

Scott asked, "Do the police think the bomb could have been meant for them? I've never heard of a pro-choice group dedicated to violence."

"But the pro-life groups see them as killers. It's all in your perspective. The police have found a group that has a connection to protests about abortions. One person was found dead in the part of the building we believe were their offices. Everybody wants to understand the connection. No one does yet."

I asked, "Anybody else who died that was connected to anything suspicious?"

"We're reasonably certain the bomber did not die in the explosion. We don't have an extra limb or anything like they did in Oklahoma City, although it's still early. One of the people who died in the copy shop had ID that showed he was a legal immigrant from Iraq. That also proves nothing."

Scott asked, "How about the employees of the clinic itself?"

"I've got nothing on that so far."

Scott told him about Gloria Dellios and her connection to clinics that had experienced attacks.

"It needs to be checked," Pulver said. "Didn't I read somewhere that over twenty-five percent of the abortion clinics have had some kind of violence occur at them this year? I suspect all of them get threats. Another thing to consider is the string of violence that happens to abortion providers every fall."

I said, "I've seen articles about that."

"We've got possible international implications," Pulver said. "I know the Canadian authorities are very interested."

"But weren't those shootings, not bombings?" Scott asked.

"The method is different, but you never know when a nut is going to escalate. Frustration builds. Violence ensues."

I said, "We heard a rumor that we were suspects. That we're being investigated by homophobic cops."

"Not that I've heard of. I can check it."

Scott asked, "Have you found out anything about that

146

Internet rumor about the Tools of Satan having a headquarters near there?"

"Nobody's even been able to confirm that a group by that name exists. The newest reports are that Braxton Thornburg was seen in the area before the explosion but not after. You've heard of him?"

I said, "Isn't he the California bomber who's supposed to have been hiding in the High Sierra for years?"

"How reliable are those reports?" Scott asked.

"No real proof yet. Just more Internet drivel."

For a few minutes we discussed the threats we'd gotten. At the end I said, "I think we could try putting ourselves out as bait. If someone is following us that closely, we could draw them out. If they thought our guards were gone, we could catch them."

Pulver said, "And if your guards were gone and these people were very good, you could be dead in seconds."

"I agree," Scott said. "It's too dangerous."

I dropped the idea.

Pulver knew no further information. We thanked him.

As we left, he told us, "Good luck, you guys. If you want to get hold of me without telling Kenny, here's my card with my private pager number. Seriously, he is your best possible defense."

McCutcheon joined us as we walked out.

"Where to?" Scott asked as McCutcheon waited in the car.

"I think we should talk to Gloria Dellios. I want to find out who else was hurt and who else died at the clinic. I knew a few of them. I'd like to see how they are. And we could ask her a few questions, such as why she just happened to be walking out of the clinic when the bomb exploded. Also, if Susan Clancey was coming to town, Gloria might have known."

18

It was late afternoon. I was hungry, and I needed some sleep. Scott was yawning as we rode.

We stopped at Carson's for Ribs on Wells Street. I had the pork chops and Scott the end cut of prime rib. Both of us ordered their famed "garbage" salad. We talked little until the end of the meal, and then mostly I was content to hear about the carpentry project Scott was working on. Simple domestic conversation was eminently soothing. We talked about paying the bills and taking his car in for a tune-up, and about a new car for me.

We picked up a paper to hunt for details about the explosion and to see if they had a list of the dead and injured. From the headlines to the final squibs, they mostly reported on the press conferences the police had been having. There were pictures of investigators standing on the debris at the site; investigators giving interviews; investigators looking solemn while standing behind politicians being reassuring. All these were crammed amid as many pictures of sobbing people as they could find. A photo of Scott helping a fireman filled half of page six of the *Sun Times*. The City Council had met in special session to offer a million-dollar reward for information leading to an arrest.

We'd been to a party at Gloria Dellios's house about six months ago. My friend who had died in the clinic, Alvana, had made sure we were invited. Dellios's phone number wasn't listed, so we couldn't call ahead. A listed phone number for an abortion provider was an open invitation to the crazed. Although with Web sites listing names and addresses, secrecy wasn't as vital as it once was.

She lived in the oddly placed apartment complex built in the middle of Fifty-fifth Street just west of Hyde Park Boulevard. We found a parking place a half block up on Dorchester Court. Her apartment was on the tenth floor and looked toward the west.

She wore an old University of Oregon sweatshirt and faded blue jeans. Her hair was pulled back and tied with a gray ribbon. Numerous wisps of hair leaked from the bow. The fading sunlight caught these strands and made it look as if her face had a wild glow around it.

She hugged me briefly. "Thank God, you're all right. What did the doctors say?" Her words were kindly, but even in those short phrases she mixed in deep sighs and pregnant pauses. She spoke listlessly, as if each syllable were a burden. It was almost painful to listen to her.

I gave her a brief summary.

We sat in a living room filled with waiting-room chic: cheap vinyl chairs with pea-soup-green seats and chrome armrests, a few Golden Books for children strewn on a nicked and scarred coffee table. A couch stuck out from a wall, dividing the living room from the dining room. The track lighting was dim. The walls were bare except for a poster advertising a woman's music festival in Seneca Falls, New York.

I pointed at the books. "You have children?"

She smiled faintly. "No. Those are for my sister's kids. They live in the neighborhood and drop by frequently. I try to keep educational activities strategically placed around the apartment. Part of the reason I moved to Chicago was to be closer to my sister and her kids. She's recently divorced, and I wanted to be supportive. We're all each other has."

I said, "I'm worried about who else might have been hurt in the explosion. We couldn't find a newspaper with a list of victims. We wanted to talk to you as well. Who besides Alvana was hurt at the clinic?"

"I'm going to miss Alvana. She was so fabulous. Always a good person to talk to. Always a voice of calm and reason." Dellios began to cry.

I remained silent as she dabbed at her eyes. I wasn't sure I could talk very well at that moment either. I knew I would miss Alvana a great deal.

After her tears stopped, she said, "I'm not sure if anyone else you know was hurt. I've seen partial lists in several papers. So many are dead." She handed me a list. I scanned it as she spoke. "We've been open seven days a week for years. We were closing in less than an hour. A few more minutes and it would have been so different. What happened there is so awful. The clinic is destroyed, and its services are desperately needed."

No one else's name besides the ones Alvana's roommate had mentioned was on the list. I asked, "Who actually owns the clinic?"

"A consortium of women doctors."

"Are the police checking to see if anyone was angry enough at one of them to blow up the whole place?"

151

"Human anger I understand," Dellios said. "Getting even, while distasteful, is a very natural response to what you see as injustice. But I just don't understand that much anger directed at one person. Would that be worth causing this kind of destruction and so much harm to so many?"

I said, "Irrational anger is in vogue. It's the emotion of the moment, and it's acceptable and encouraged in some segments of the population."

Dellios said, "I don't get why some men are so angry and concerned about women they don't know who are making a choice. I think the heart of the problem is some men cannot relinquish power and control over women."

"Do either of those things really matter now?" Scott asked. "Whatever the reason, and there are probably many, a lot of people have died because of some nut."

Dellios said, "All of us who work in such places live a life of fear. So many people I care very much about have been hurt in very many ways." She reached for a box of tissues on a nearby table, dabbed at her eyes, and tossed it into a wastebasket already filled to near the top with other tissue. "I wasn't crazed after the explosion that night because I was so busy. I wish I had something to work on now. Anything to get my mind off this horror." She pulled out another tissue and used it. "I hate it when women cry, but I'm not sure what other reaction makes sense. If I get angry about what happened, I'm just as bad as whoever did this. If I just feel sad, I feel like I'm betraying the women who died and the cause I believe in. I want to fight, but I don't know how or who. There is just too much hate."

"You're in one of the most dangerous professions," I said. "It can't be easy living with the constant pressure and threats."

"I've been a lot of places and tried to help a lot of people.

Yet, some people think I don't value human life because of what I do. They couldn't be more wrong. I hope the police catch who did this. I want to see justice done, not get revenge. I just would like to be able to ask whoever did it, 'Why?' "

I said, "The only answer that makes sense is hatred, distorted, unreasoning hatred. All other answers are inadequate, and that one is incomprehensible to rational people. Have the police been able to tell you anything?"

"Whenever I haven't been at the hospital, I've been at the police station. I've gone over as many threats as I can remember. None of them stood out. We kept a log of any calls and letters, but I can't imagine it survived the fire."

"The police will probably be coming by to ask more questions."

"Why? I've already told them everything."

How do you say nicely, you yourself are going to be coming under suspicion because of some data a reporter happened to stumble upon? I said simply, "We were talking to a reporter who knew some data about the clinics you've worked at. They've had lots of troubles."

"All clinics have had lots of troubles."

"These seemed to have major problems while you were on the staff."

I'm not much of a judge of people's expressions, and I'm wrong often enough to be humble about it, but I thought I saw dismay followed by fear.

She rose to her feet. I figured she was about to toss us out. I was wrong. She strode behind the couch and ran her hand over it's faded and cracked plastic. For an uncomfortably long time she didn't look at either one of us.

Finally she whispered, "I was wondering when someone was going to notice. Years ago a friend of mine worked at a succession of clinics. Within a month after she started in three straight places, they were victims of acid attacks."

I knew antiabortion activists would pour butyric acid in mail slots or through small openings they'd drilled in the walls. The acid is used in perfumes and disinfectants. Undiluted it smells like rotten eggs. It irritates the skin and the respiratory system. It does an annoying, although seldom a significant, amount of damage. The clinics often had to close until hazardous-materials teams got rid of the residue.

I asked, "Did someone connect your friend with the crimes?"

"A woman reporter in Sacramento, California, was doing a profile on a clinic where my friend worked. The reporter started asking questions about her background. My friend figured out what she was after and quit the next day. She went back to school to get her law degree. She didn't want the pressure and the insult of being investigated."

"Did she do it?" I asked.

"No. She had solid alibis for two of the occasions."

"So why didn't she stick to her story?" Scott asked.

"Simply being accused is bad enough. I had a friend who set off the theft alarm on her way out of one of those chain bookstores. She had her receipt in her hand. The clerks apologized profusely. They gave her a free gift certificate, but she was too humiliated to ever go back. She never wanted to risk setting off an alarm again. To this day she won't shop in a store that has one of those. It causes her no end of hassles, but she's sticking to her guns."

"Isn't that kind of an overreaction?" Scott asked.

"To her it wasn't. She felt debased and frightened." Dellios walked around to the front of the couch and paced for a few moments. "I've been worried about someone making the link between all those places and my working there. I had no

154

way to stop the connection being made. Much of the time I've felt like my career and my life were hanging by a thread."

"Why didn't you just quit?" Scott asked. "There are other ways to serve the causes you care about."

"I imagine the reasons I didn't quit are very similar to reasons you didn't quit playing baseball."

Scott said, "I understand that."

Dellios continued, "I didn't bomb my own clinic. I have no reason to. I am not a murderer."

I asked, "What are you going to say when the police want to know how it was that you were outside in a safe spot?"

"You mean just like you're doing now?"

"Yeah." I felt a little embarrassed at the boldness of the question, but I couldn't think of another way to word it.

She brushed at some of the stray strands of hair around her face. She pulled her sweatshirt closer around her torso. She began slowly. "I'm a simple person, really. I believe in nonviolence. I grew up as the kid in the family who was always trying to make peace with my brothers and sisters, with the kids in the neighborhood, between the kids at school. It seemed so easy, so natural. Now I carry a gun. I keep a shotgun here under my bed. Me, who's been a pacifist since high school, me owning a gun! I have a state-of-the-art burglar-alarm system surrounding this shabby apartment. I have a fire alarm in each room. I know antichoice fanatics probably wouldn't attack just this one place, but look what they did to that city block. And they've found the home addresses and assassinated those doctors." She sighed deeply. "My sister keeps telling me to get out of the business, but women need me. They need to have a place where they can feel safe to exercise their choices." She stopped and stared into the middle distance for several moments.

I asked, "What happened at those other clinics?"

155

"The police never caught anyone. Just like whoever's been targeting and killing abortion providers here and in Canada. I thought things would get better after we won that racketeering case a few years ago."

She was referring to a case brought by the National Organization for Women and two clinics in Delaware and Wisconsin against two antiabortion groups and their leaders.

She went on, "We won the case, but it was like winning the battle and losing the war. The attacks never really lessened. I am not willing to sacrifice my sanity and my entire life. I have no clinic to return to. I am not applying for another job in one. I'm getting out."

I asked, "Do you always leave at that time on a Saturday?"

"Why are you so concerned?"

"I think my concern is natural."

"You sound like you're investigating."

"I was injured in the blast. My friend died. Alvana's child is still not out of danger. Scott and I have been under threat. My personal life and public life have merged to the point of constant danger. I want to put a stop to as much of that as possible. I'm not ready to walk away yet. Before I retire to a lead-lined bunker, I'm going to fight back."

Dellios said, "There's only so much a person can take. Accusing me isn't going to help. I'm no threat to either of you. I barely know Scott. I only know you from your part-time work at the clinic. I'm certainly sympathetic to you as a gay couple, and I'm not a killer."

I said, "We heard a rumor that Susan Clancey was supposed to be coming to town."

Dellios made a little *eep* noise and twittered her fingers around her throat. "I don't know where you could have heard that."

The intercom buzzed. She walked to the switch, flicked it on, and asked, "Who's there?"

"Detective Jantoro, Chicago police. I need to talk with you again, Ms. Dellios."

She buzzed him in. Before she opened the apartment door, she inspected him through the security peephole. Jantoro entered, nodded hello to us, and said, "I need to talk to Ms. Dellios alone."

She made no protest and neither did we.

In the entrance to the apartment house Scott said, "She didn't answer your questions about why she left when she did."

"I know. The fact that she wouldn't tell us why she left makes it suspicious to me. Not only that, she looked panicked when I asked her about Clancey."

Scott said, "If she set the bomb, wouldn't she have been farther away when it went off?"

"I guess."

"And if she was planning to blow up that block, wouldn't she have already had an excuse for leaving? She'd know she'd need one. I think her lack of an excuse shows that she didn't do it. Whoever was crazy enough to set off that bomb was also bright enough to do a lot of complex planning."

"You could be right." I was tired. "Let's go home. We can call that reporter's contact on the East Coast."

19

As we took the elevator to Scott's penthouse, I said, "You know, we could just not call McCutcheon tomorrow and go off on our own."

"You can if you want," Scott said, "I have no intention of going around town without him. You can decide how brave you are and how much danger you're willing to risk. I, for one, think we need to use him."

We called the East Coast. As the phone rang, I eased into an overstuffed chair. It felt wonderful. I was more tired than I thought.

Thieme's contact, Toby Ratshinski had a deep voice. I pictured a lumberjack. I explained about Thieme and what he'd told us about McCutcheon.

Ratshinski's skepticism disappeared at the mention of Thieme's name. It was quickly replaced with curiosity about us. "This is really Tom Mason? The guy who was on all those talk shows?"

I assured him it was and that Scott was on the extension.

"Wow. This is great. I admire you guys so much. I'd be happy to do what I can for you."

"What were you doing in Bosnia?" I asked.

"I was the lowest rung on the reporting ladder for the *Washington Post*. I was willing to do anything to have a career in journalism. If it took going to Bosnia, I figured it was worth the risk. Better than reporting on school board and zoning meetings in the farthest suburbs around Washington, D.C. How will my knowledge about Bosnia help you guys?"

I said, "We heard you got beat up in Bosnia."

"I sure did."

"We're interested in the guy who did it."

"A nasty, tough son of a bitch."

"Angus Thieme thought the guy looked like the owner of the security firm we've hired. We're trying to be sure of his identity. Could you describe the man you made a pass at?"

"A college-wrestler type. Very wiry, lithe, not too tall. I forget the color of his eyes."

"What happened?"

"I was in this absolute hellhole of a town. We'd been threatened by police, security officers, and the armies on both sides in the conflict. We were constantly afraid for our lives. A group of us had pretty much decided to beat it out of there. This guy was with us all the time. No one knew what his job really was. He wasn't a reporter. Everybody assumed he was with the CIA. One night I was drinking. I was far from home, scared, and lonely. He was a stud. We were in a war zone."

He paused. I thought I heard him take a sip of liquid. In a moment, he continued, "We talked intimately for hours. He sat closer to me than need required. He invited me to stay overnight at his place."

When I was dating, guys had to practically spell out in

neon their interest or lack of same. A blatant grab of the crotch is a clear message, but I was never good at picking up on the more subtle nonverbal cues.

Ratshinski continued, "At the entrance to a dark, narrow, and treacherously steep stairway, I put my hand on his butt. He lost his temper. He switched from friendly and affectionate to a raging madman in an instant. He literally picked me up and threw me into the street. I'm not a very big guy, but that was unbelievable. He began pounding on me. I think he might have killed me except a jeep-load of MPs happened by. They made him stop, but they didn't arrest him. I had no one to really complain to. The local authorities were a joke. Appeal to our military was a ludicrous idea. Anyway, as far as I could see, he wasn't under their jurisdiction."

"We need to be sure this is the same guy. Can you think of any way we could know that it was him? Your description isn't very specific. Thieme's tentative identification is all we have to go on."

"I know when I grabbed him, he didn't pull away for a few seconds. After he began hitting me, I managed to grab him. For someone who acted like he wasn't interested, his dick sure seemed to be."

Scott said, "Any scars, tattoos, obvious ticks?" I caught a hint of sarcasm beginning to creep into his voice.

"I don't remember. He was sexy. I saw him taking a piss by the side of the road once. I think he was uncut."

This was not going to be enough. "We need something positive we can use."

"I'll try and think of something."

After we hung up, Scott said, "That was unhelpful."

"Should we have asked him to come to Chicago? We can afford to put him up for the night in a hotel."

"Do you really want to do that?" Scott asked.

"We could if we have to."

"Do you think that's reasonable at this time?"

"I'm not sure what's reasonable and neither are you. You're the one who's going from frantically willing to spend a million dollars to see what's at the bottom of this to being hesitant and unsure about what we should do."

"I am restating my official position that I want to take us away from all this forever."

"You're going to quit pitching? I'm going to quit teaching? Are we going to hide so completely that we never see our families? Even if we did leave, we'd still be living mostly in fear. All that makes sense to you?"

"It doesn't have to make sense. It just has to be safe and secure."

"And if only one of us goes?"

"I'm not going without you."

I began to stand up, but I felt a mild wave of dizziness. I grabbed the arm of the chair.

Scott hurried over. "Are you all right?"

"Just a little woozy. I want a night's sleep in my own bed without fear of terrorists. Let tomorrow's dread fend for itself."

I called the school's answering machine and confirmed that I would not be in for the rest of the week. I had a doctor's note stating the need for me to rest. Scott checked the messages with the service as I got ready for bed. I turned off all the lights except the small reading lamp on my side of the bed. I usually read something every night before I fall asleep. That didn't feel right tonight. While the wrangling we'd been doing didn't count as an official fight, I was uncomfortable. I still needed to talk to him. One of the few bits of wisdom my parents told me that stuck was never go to sleep angry. I've found they were right.

162

I sat up in bed with my back propped up against the pillows as he finished brushing his teeth. I heard the brush rattle when he put it in the holder. He switched off the light. As he crossed the room, he was lit by the glow of the city below. Half his face and torso were in shadow. His white briefs shimmered in the silent radiance. Living at the top of a building on Lake Shore Drive means there is always light of some kind coming through the windows. I was struck as I so often am by his athletic grace and rugged beauty. He crawled into bed and sat up next to me. I took his hand.

"I respect your fears," I began. "I don't want my own dread to control my life. I don't know what to do about it. I can't see running for the rest of my life. You're right. If we went far away for quite a while, I think people would begin to forget that we exist. The concept of a private island with a bevy of pool boys to attend to our every need has a certain charm. I just don't think it's realistic. I don't think I could do it. I know I don't want to do it."

"I'm still scared," Scott responded. "Every unguarded moment brings back the picture of what I saw outside that clinic. I don't want that to be us. I wish I could stop the dreams at night. I wish I could stop the memories during the day. But bad as those feelings are, I'm more worried about you and me. I don't know what to do."

He pulled me closer and put his arm around me. I felt his warmth and closeness and caught the mint aroma from his toothpaste. I breathed deeply.

"I'm not sure what to do," I said. "It feels right to be trying to stop these threats against us. Here in bed, our connection to what happened at the clinic seems more remote. We've got a small piece of the world to fix. We're not safe. Someone has made threats. That note in the hospital and someone being able to get that close scares me. I think we have a very specific person who needs to be stopped. I think we should still be questioning people."

"Do you really believe it's possible for us to find out who it is? Look at the all the investigating the police did."

"But we didn't do any."

He said, "We aren't more qualified than they are."

There was no sarcasm in his voice. This was different from the wrangling earlier. His sonorous voice with its slight Southern drawl murmuring through it rumbled softly into my ear. I snuggled into his shoulder and side. The hair on his chest made a wonderful nest to burrow against. I felt safe and warm and comfortable.

"I know we aren't more qualified, but I think we have a more direct concern than the police. We've trusted everybody else to make us safe. We may not be able to do much, but with a little persistence and a lot of luck, we might be able to do something."

"I hope you're right."

"Me too." After several moments of silence, I said, "I'm getting really sleepy." Neither of us moved. I felt myself nodding off and my head drooping on his shoulder. That's when my memories of returning to the scene came back. I thought of Alan Redpath lying in the hospital. The sense of fortuitous escape crept into my mind until it was overwhelming. My eyes opened. I felt my heart pound.

Scott yawned. "You okay?" he muttered.

I nodded that I was, but I wasn't. I hadn't had this kind of memory since my days in the marines. It was as unpleasant now as it had been then. All the helplessness and sense of simple luck ruling my life rushed back. It felt as if I were falling from a great height. I'd dreamed this more times than I've ever admitted to Scott. I'd be falling with all kinds of time to think about not having a parachute. About not having a net below me. There was never anything I could do to stop the ground from rushing ever closer. Nothing that would stop the ground from being very hard. Nothing that would stop the coming of death.

I was alive only because I was too annoyed to stay and argue with a woman who was now dead. Because a little boy had dropped a ball. There was no decision I could have made, no action I could have taken, to change what had happened.

◣ 20 ◢

Morning's discomforting light arrived far sooner than I wished. While Scott was in the shower, the phone rang. The service had a message from Angus Thieme. I called him at his hotel. His militia expert could meet us in an hour at the Breakfast Club on Hubbard Street.

I told Scott. He pulled back the shower curtain and said, "You should call McCutcheon so he can go with us."

With some reluctance I did so. McCutcheon said he'd have the car outside in half an hour. I wondered if he was ever late or ever held up in traffic or ever anything less than perfect. I wished I trusted him more.

I showered and shaved quickly. The weather was cooler so I wore a sweater Scott had bought for me in Ireland two winters ago. He wore a University of Arizona sweatshirt.

The Breakfast Club is an amazingly pleasant place to have breakfast. If you go, try the scones. They are unimaginably good and a delightful bonus after the superior main fare.

A bald, portly figure matching Thieme's description

stood outside on the corner. There was no line waiting on a Wednesday. We were seated immediately. Owen Harvey looked to be in his late fifties or early sixties. The bottom portion of his left earlobe was oddly jagged as if it might have been cut off by an unsharpened knife or bitten through and ripped away. I had to stop myself from staring at this oddity.

After we ordered, Harvey said, "Angus says you boys are in a bit of a fix. He asked me to help you out."

"Who do you work for?" Scott asked.

"Officially I'm a freelancer, but mostly I work for United States government agencies. If you want identification, you're out of luck."

Again, I was hesitant about trusting a stranger, but what could we do? Have confidence in a stranger or get no information. I didn't see any other way out. I said, "We're suspicious about a guy named Ken McCutcheon, who was using the name of Forandi in Bosnia. Also, if you could tell us anything else about the bombing investigation, we'd appreciate it. I was in the explosion. We've also been personally threatened." Scott and I gave him details about our problem.

When we finished, Harvey said, "People employ me mostly for background information. Antiabortion protesters are one of my specialties. McCutcheon's name has come up on the periphery of a number of my other investigations. I've never been able to ascertain if he's a problem or a solution. Maybe a little of both. I'm sorry I don't know more. I know nothing about his activities in Bosnia."

Scott asked, "Can you tell us anything about that banquet with all those protesters in attendance?"

"I have no indication that any of them set the bomb. A lot of the fanatics started out as perfectly nice people who just got themselves in deeper. Much of the impetus has come from members of the Catholic Church, which I hasten to add,

168

as an institution, always condemns violence against the clinics and the workers."

"Do you think they're sincere?"

"I have absolutely no proof or even a slight suspicion that the Catholic Church is leading a vast conspiracy to destroy abortion clinics or murder people. The cardinals and bishops don't go in for guns and bombs. They have enough clout by picking up the phone and talking to politicians. Violence could put that power at risk. Nor do I have any reason to believe that any of the mainstream or radical-right Protestant churches have anything to do with organizing violence."

Scott asked, "What about the atmosphere they create that gives aid and comfort to those who do the violence?"

"All of that is politics," Harvey replied, "not forensics. Not hard data. People can be felled by any kind of crazy idea. If I get involved in the debate between freedom of speech and death threats, I get nowhere. I stick to real facts."

"What can you tell us?" I asked.

"I found out some information on the protesters outside the clinic. I have passed this on to the police, of course, and to Angus, who I have worked with before. We have been of benefit to each other."

Our food arrived. We ate for a few minutes in silence. Then Harvey said, "Most of the people who protest outside the Human Services Clinic are simply good people drawn to a cause they believe in very deeply. A hard-core group of about seven were the ones who really kept it alive. Of those seven, two are known to be prone to violence. They are suspected in three clinic incidents in Florida and one in Seattle."

"Why weren't they targets of investigations before?" Scott asked.

"They were. The key word here is *suspected*. No one has been able to prove anything. Some of the pro-life people kill and run. However, these folks have managed to stay above ground and beyond the reach of the law. After an incident of violence they're the bunch that claim no responsibility. The kind who yell 'Fire!' in a crowded theater and claim to be innocent after so many die."

"They can really get away with that?" Scott asked.

"Mostly they do."

I asked, "Do protesters really move around that much?"

"Oh, yes. They're a lot like people who used to go to Grateful Dead concerts. They travel from one hot-button spot to another. They hear about a big protest being planned, and they all hurry out to wherever it is. The two I mentioned have been in and out of town a lot recently. That kind of travel on their part is not inherently suspicious, but I believe the authorities are trying to be sure of exactly where they were when."

Scott said, "You mean finding out if they rented a truck like the one used in the explosion."

"So far no one has a lead on that. No one around the country has reported one missing."

"How hard can it be to buy your own?" Scott asked. "Or pick up a used semi at a used-semi sale? There must be such things."

"They're still trying to trace it," Harvey said. "The truck in the Oklahoma bombing was traced because they found part of the axle with a serial number on it. Nobody has reported finding any such thing here."

I asked, "Does either one of the two people you're talking about have a background in explosives?"

"I'm not aware that either one is a bomb expert. You don't need a background in explosives anymore. All you need is a computer hooked up to the Internet. It helps if you know some other crazies, but that is not essential."

I said, "Instant worldwide communication, a boon for the new millennium."

"I use it all the time," Harvey said. "It's easier to keep up with the crazies that way. You can share information with legitimate sources. You've heard the rumor about Braxton Thornburg?"

"Yeah."

"I'm working on the assumption that he was here. We'll see how far that gets me. The two people I've been talking about are Omega Collins and Edward Eggleston. You may have seen pictures of Eggleston on TV news or in the paper. He's the emaciated one with the big nose. He tries to get himself arrested, and as soon as the cops touch him, he screams brutality. His father was a precinct worker in the Democratic organization on the southeast side of Chicago. Edward was an altar boy, Cub Scout, Boy Scout, Eagle Scout, honor student, by all accounts a teenage saint."

I said, "His peers probably hated him."

"He was voted most likely to succeed in his senior year of high school. He started to get radicalized in college. He is said to have talked the girl he was dating out of having an abortion."

Scott said, "Can you blame him for wanting to save a child that was his?"

Harvey said, "In fact, it wasn't his own kid. He and the girl didn't have sex. He was saving himself for marriage."

"How'd she feel about all this?"

"They were married the day he graduated from college. She had the kid a few weeks before the ceremony. Since then they've had three more kids in five years. I'm told he is a doting father to all four children."

Scott asked, "How does he pay the bills if he's out protesting?"

"He's officially the head of the splinter group nominally sponsoring the protests." Harvey glanced at a piece of paper. "They call themselves Jesus' Family."

"Never heard of them," Scott said.

"It's just the name for their umbrella group so they can have a tax-exempt status, and so people have a name and address to send donations to. The address is a post office box rented by Eggleston."

"Could he really be the bomber?" Scott asked. "He sounds more like he should be posing for pedestals."

"After incredible amounts of hard work, I managed to get hold of all the Web sites he's visited on his computer. They included lots of places that sold guns and talked about bombs."

"I thought all of that was classified," Scott said. "Don't the on-line companies get in trouble for giving out that kind of information?"

"If you've got a computer on-line," Harvey said, "I can probably find out just about anything I want about what you've been doing. Not everything, but more than you'd ever want me to."

"You're not just bragging?" Scott asked.

"Nope."

I asked, "Who is this Omega person?"

"Omega Collins is a piece of work." Harvey mopped up the remnants of his whipped cream with the last bits of scone, took a sip of coffee, and then explained, "Before I began investigating her, Omega used to be a great deal of a mystery woman. She'd travel from city to city and didn't seem to have a permanent address. She had no visible means of support. She liked to keep an aura of intrigue and danger about her."

"Is she dangerous?" Scott asked.

"I think so."

I asked, "Is there any evidence she was involved in any bombings?"

"No," Harvey admitted. "It's been mostly a pattern of attacks in cities she's been in. Attacks that start when she arrives and stop when she goes."

Scott said, "That sounds like the pattern with Gloria Dellios."

"Who is she?" Harvey asked.

I explained.

Harvey said, "I've never heard of her, although that doesn't mean anything. Actually working inside the clinic would be unique. I agree with you that it doesn't seem likely that a true believer would be able to be that close to that which they most despise, but I'll look into her as well."

I said, "A smart terrorist could become aware of patterns of behavior among clinic workers and time their activities on an innocent person's schedule."

Harvey looked thoughtful. "Very possible. Proving a conspiracy has been done, but it's tough. The abortion rights groups have won all kind of judgments and injunctions against various protesters, but the victories in court often don't do a lot of good. The pro-life crowd isn't generally very wealthy. True believers seldom are. What good does it do to win a million-dollar settlement against someone who hasn't even got a savings account?"

"Or have divested themselves of all assets beforehand," Scott commented.

"What did you find out about her?" I asked.

"She comes from a poor family in the hills of Kentucky. No one is sure where or why she decided that abortion was her cause. She dropped out of high school about ten years ago. Her only listed address is the family farm, but she often disappears from there, sometimes for months at a time. They claim not to know where she is. She's barely five feet tall and weighs less than a hundred pounds, but she's got enough of a temper to fuel several religious wars. I get rumors of a violent home life, but I can't get anyone in her hometown to open up about her. A real hills-and-hollers you're-a-stranger-you're-the-enemy mentality. She's tough. If you see a picture on the news of a woman yelling shrill obscenities outside a clinic, it's probably her. You must have seen the famous picture of her, by herself, facing down a line of marching lesbians in Houston a couple of years ago?"

I nodded, then asked, "But she's done nothing provably criminal?"

"Not so far."

"Would it do any good for us to talk to either one of them?"

"You ever talked to one of these people?" Harvey asked.

"No."

"You would get bored really fast. Listening to them is like hearing a one-note symphony, not a lot of fun and very, very irritating very, very quickly. You guys are too well-known. I doubt if you'd get past introducing yourselves."

Scott asked, "Can't you get them away from their fellow workers and the television cameras? Maybe they're different once the floodlights are turned off."

"I've never known them to be."

Scott said, "They must pay the bills, talk about child care and grocery shopping, buy toilet paper. There must be a human connection."

"You'd think so," Harvey said. "I've had coffee with some of them. I even ate a burger with a guy who went out and assassinated a doctor the next week. He seemed perfectly normal to me. They don't wear neon letter *A*'s on their shirt-fronts."

I asked, "If we decide to talk to them, can you give us any advice about the approach we should take?"

Harvey shrugged. "If you get close enough to introduce yourself, speak calmly and don't excite them."

Scott said, "You sound like we need to treat them like they're wounded animals or criminally insane."

"They are certainly not the first and are probably not the latter. I just know I would never back one of them into a corner. They combine the naïveté and viciousness of true believers to as great a degree as the most rabid Islamic fundamentalist or IRA terrorist."

I asked, "Who else would you recommend that we talk to?"

"Depends what you're trying to do. For example, I think it would be a waste of time talking to any of the people at the banquet. While they could have used a remote-control bomb or a timer, I heard they all have alibis for the time of the explosion. If you're trying to solve the bombing, I'd say forget it. You don't have the resources. You'd be surprised how many of these bombers get away. It's true international terrorists are frequently given safe havens by hostile governments, but more often the chase ends more in frustration. Look how long it took to find the Unabomber. Thornburg's been running for years. If you're trying to deal with who is threatening you, I'm not sure what to tell you."

"We've got to try something. I'm not sure where to turn next."

"You've got Angus Thieme on your side. He enjoys the good things in life a little too much now to be as effective as he was in the old days. Still, Angus is better than most. Do not underestimate Angus's goodwill. Having the liberal press on your side is no bad thing. He got me to talk to you."

We thanked him and left. Outside, Scott said, "Are you really going to try to talk to one of those people?"

"We might."

McCutcheon leaned against his Hummer about thirty feet from us. He'd been as polite, efficient, and correct as he always was.

Scott asked, "Why are Kearn, Thieme, and Harvey being so nice to us?"

"Kearn is interested because he sees us as part of a possible ticket to a national news desk in New York or maybe his own cable-television show. He's pretty enough that it could happen. Maybe they all have sympathy for us because of who we are."

Scott said, "Three straight men who are suddenly at the forefront in helping two gay guys is a tough concept for me to swallow. And don't say I'm having cognitive dissonance. Save that for your friends at school."

"I simply try to describe what I see."

"Leave that to the existentialist."

"What?"

"Skip it. The point is, why are these people being nice to us?"

"I don't know. Shouldn't we talk to some of your friends who had McCutcheon as a client and see if we can find out more about him?"

"Nobody knew anything then, why would they now?"

"He must come from somewhere real. He can't have appeared out of nowhere."

"I agree, but believe me, no one knows."

"A disgruntled former worker would be good."

"I don't know any. I've only met the guys who guard me."

"We could go to his offices."

"And what, beat down the door, which is probably unlocked, beat the truth out of employees who may know as little as we do?"

"Let's ask him," I suggested.

"It's that simple?"

"I'd be happy to have a better suggestion." Scott didn't have one.

We strolled over to McCutcheon. He gazed at us evenly. I began, "We want to find out if you are a threat to us. We have absolutely no clue as to how to proceed. We thought we'd start with you."

McCutcheon smiled. "Isn't that sort of like the hound asking the fox for tips?"

"Aren't you willing to help us clear you from the suspect list? Only if you were one of the ones conspiring against us would you feel the need to keep your mouth shut."

"It's taken you a while to get to that insight."

"Sorry, I've been unconscious. Sometimes that slows me down. We could use some background. Why don't you tell anyone about yourself? What's the point of being so mysterious about who you are and where you came from?"

"The point is, it's nobody's business."

"But why? You may not owe us an explanation, but can't you see it would make a difference to us?"

"Why don't we get into the car and then we can talk."

I sat in the front with McCutcheon. Scott was in the back.

"I don't think telling you is going to help much, because who I am and why I am the way I am is not going to tell you who is a threat to you. I don't know why you would believe me. At any rate, an outline. I was born in Green Bay, Wisconsin. I'm thirty, although everyone thinks I'm younger. I've never been married. I've had sex with men and women, although I pretty much prefer not to have sex at all."

"Why not?"

"To me sex implies a relationship. I don't want a commitment. I want to do what I want when I want."

"But you come whenever we call."

"But that's my job. It's what I want to do." He resumed his narrative. "I joined the service out of high school. I was in the military police. I proved valuable and was recruited into a special branch for covert activities."

"The CIA?"

"Not officially."

"Were you in Bosnia?" I asked. "Did you attack that gay guy?"

"I beat the crap out of him because he was about to be assassinated, and I couldn't stop the crowd that was going to kill him. By the time I incapacitated the simple twit, there were a lot of MPs and an American army ambulance on hand. It saved his life."

"Who wanted to kill him?"

"Some Serbs he'd seen killing women and children. They are not nice people."

"You were forced to beat him up?" I hoped I sounded as incredulous as I felt.

"Were you there?"

"No."

"I can tell you this. If I wanted to kill him, he'd be dead. You're asking me for my story. I'm telling you. If you choose to doubt it, I don't much care. I told you I didn't think it would help. You know something about me. How has that helped you be less threatened?"

"Maybe it means for a little while I'll be less inclined to think you're one of the people out to get us."

"Fine."

Scott asked, "Have you ever been a member of any militia group?"

"Nope."

We sat in silence for several moments. McCutcheon asked, "Where do you want to go?"

"Borini and Faslo," Scott said. "Let's see if they have something for us."

We drove to the Sears Tower. Borini was in and agreed to see us. I was introduced. McCutcheon waited in the hall.

I began, "I was surprised when my partner told me he had hired your firm. My understanding is you've had a discrimination suit filed against you by a gay man you fired."

"The case was brought and dismissed. The person in question was an incompetent nitwit. That's why he was fired."

"You mind if we talk to him?"

"You can find his name in the court transcript so it's public knowledge so I don't mind giving it to you."

"Are you homophobic?"

"We took Mr. Carpenter's case."

"But that doesn't answer my question."

"Do you want to know what we've found out?"

"You've got something?" Scott asked.

"A little. A description. All the employees of the hospital check out as nonthreatening. Only one of them said he noticed someone who might have been suspicious. He saw a male in his early twenties who could have simply been visiting someone. He described a smooth-complexioned guy who wore a cap without any logo, a red blazer, and black tennis shoes. The employee saw this person coming out of your lover's room. You had so many visitors, it was hard to tell who belonged and who didn't. They need to get a better control on that place."

Scott said, "I don't remember anybody dressed like that."

"I think that lead is about all you're going to get."

And that's all we got. We left. I didn't remind Scott about wasting his money on a wild-goose chase since that's what we were on ourselves.

Outside, I said, "We need to find out more about who died in the explosion. Do we try Kearn or Pulver?"

Scott shrugged. "Maybe Kearn."

We stopped at the hospital to see Alan Redpath, Alvana's son. He was still unconscious. He looked to be hooked up to more machines than he had been before. I found Alvana's brother, Oliver, a man I'd met on several occasions. He was younger than she, but a throwback to the sixties. Normally he wore tie-dyed T-shirts and bell-bottom jeans. Today his long hair was pulled back in a ponytail. He wore clothes that actually looked as if they'd been laundered recently. He'd bathed and put on deodorant, two activities often lacking in his hygiene.

"What's the prognosis?" I asked.

"They don't know," he said. "No one knows. I'm frightened."

We comforted him as best we could. Alvana's parents were dead. Her brother was her closest living relative. Alvana had been artificially inseminated. She never wanted to be hassled by the father of her child or have any interference from him in the way she reared the boy.

On the way back to the penthouse, we picked up Scott's car. Back home, I called the service to check our messages. We had one from Myrtle Mae. The computer voice gave the time and date of the message, a half hour earlier. The cryptic note from the voice mail said, "I hate having to go through these damn machines. I don't know why you can't give your number out to people you trust. This is so annoying. I need to talk to you. The police want to question me again." After a thump or bump in the background, he said, "Oh, well, do you have access to the videotapes from the television coverage? Do you know anyone who could get them? I've got to get those tapes. Don't trust anyone! Don't bother to call. No matter what time you get this, come over immediately."

I had Scott listen to the message.

"He's hysterical about something," Scott said. "Sounds like normal Myrtle Mae behavior to me. He gets blitheringly emotional about something that turns out to be inaccurate if not totally untrue. When he gets hyper, we're all supposed to dance to his tune. I wonder what he told the police. He wanted a butch one to interview him. Maybe he's in love and needs us to witness their wedding ceremony."

"I think it sounded important. I think we should go over there." Despite Myrtle Mae's message, I tried to call him. No one answered.

Scott called McCutcheon's number and arranged for one of the guards to accompany us.

Scott grumbled for most of the trip to Myrtle Mae's. "It's not going to be important. It's going to be melodramatic, gossipy, and silly. He's going to be condescending and insufferable."

"Try to hold back," I said. "Maybe you can get in touch with how you really feel."

"I hate him."

"You could give it a rest." I was a little fed up with Scott's antagonism toward Myrtle Mae. I was a little sharper with him than I intended. Instead of responding, he remained silent the rest of the way.

◣ 21 ◢

I genuinely liked Myrtle Mae. I get as frustrated as Scott does about the inordinate amount of press coverage drag queens get, but I don't care if people want to wear drag, three-piece business suits, or run through the streets naked. I want to know if they are kindly, friendly, and can get the job done. I also don't care if gay or straight people run to the current crop of movies featuring high drag. Scott refuses to go to any of them. The point isn't who has the most friends who do drag. I enjoyed *Priscilla, Queen of the Desert*. I hated *The Birdcage*. Neither the producers, actors, nor director had called to get my opinion of any of them. Early in our relationship Scott and I attended a drag show at the Baton Show Lounge. Scott sure looked as if he had a great time at that famed venue. I know I did.

Myrtle Mae was a good person. He wasn't some lonely old queen, applying makeup in a tawdry, ill-lit back room of some seedy dive on Division Street. He was a vital human being with a great many friends who had made a lot of difference in the lives of gay people in Chicago. He had more gay pride than a closetful of prim and proper, gray-suited A-gays. It also didn't hurt that he had a stock portfolio most people would have to win the lottery to match.

I'd been to his place frequently for meetings, but more often to take care of his plants and the cats whenever he took a vacation. When you entered his condominium on Lincoln Park West, you expected gay gothic. What you got was floor-to-ceiling dark mahogany in the foyer, living room, and dining room. He had two or three pieces of antique furniture, an elegant love seat with a Shaker chair at each end. An immense teak dining-room table dominated the vast space in front of a window that looked out over Lincoln Park to the lake. Each wall had one perfectly lit watercolor of a pastoral, Midwestern farm scene. The bedroom looked like something thrown out from the worst excesses of the harem sets of an Arabian Nights horror movie. The mess was unshakable by anything less than a magnitude-eight earthquake. In the public areas he had a housekeeper in once a week to eliminate any possible clutter. He owned the entire fourth floor. As large as his building was, there were only five tenants, one per floor. His place was worth at least three-quarters of a million.

Outside his building on Lincoln Park West, we met Brandon Kearn. He looked as dapper and handsome as ever.

"How come you're here?" I asked.

"I got a rumor that a guy in this building, Bryce Bennet, was going to be questioned by the police a second time."

So Kearn was after Myrtle Mae too.

"We told the cops he'd been in the Fattatuchis' deli earlier that night. He was supposed to be interviewed."

"I don't think he knew anything," Scott added. "He had an overrated sense of his own importance. He's the type who

184

gets hysterical over rumors. When they don't turn out to be true, he doesn't apologize. He just goes on to the next fatuous rumor."

Kearn said, "I heard he was going to be taken down to the station."

"He was a suspect?" I asked.

"I don't know. I got the rumor. My sources say he's not in any police station in the city. I hurried down here in the hopes of catching up with him before they got him."

"The cops would be here waiting for him, wouldn't they?" Scott asked. "If they think he knows something, they'd come get him pretty quick."

I shrugged. "Let's go up and see."

We dialed his number from the phone down in the lobby. No one answered.

"We can't just break in," Kearn said.

"I have a key," I said.

"Why do you have a key?" Kearn asked.

I explained about taking care of the plants and cats. I unlocked the door and we took the elevator up to the fourth floor. We entered the apartment. It was amazingly still. One of the cats rubbed up against Scott's leg. Kids and critters take to him. Half the time when I would come to feed the cats, they'd hiss at me. Frankly, I'm not all that good with plants either. I suspect they'd complain about me if they could.

I detected a faint odor of a gun's having been fired. "Don't touch anything," I whispered. I led the way as we stepped into the living room. Everything was as pristinely neat as ever. We carefully checked the den, library, and kitchen. The opera *Carmen* was just finishing on the CD player. As usual Myrtle Mae had stuffed his one-hundred-slot CD player full. It was on number seventeen. This was no guarantee of how long he'd been home. He started in random places and often programmed it to play random selections.

In his bedroom we found one of the cats crouched on the bed. He was warily watching the body on the floor.

One ghastly smear of blood covered the rug behind Myrtle Mae's head. Another drenched the side of the bedspread. One entry hole gaped in his forehead and another just above his left ear.

We all stood there and stared. The cat jumped off the bed and scooted out of the room. Myrtle Mae wore a long-sleeve, white shirt, dark blue tie, and bright yellow, baggy boxer shorts over a pair of panty hose. Myrtle Mae might want to appear outwardly butch to the cops, but he'd wear his panty hose underneath as a statement of rebellion.

"My God," Scott said.

Kearn turned nearly white. "That's one dead drag queen."

We waited in the downstairs hallway for the cops to arrive.

"What's the story on this guy?" Kearn asked as we waited.

I gave him a brief outline of Myrtle Mae's life.

"He doesn't sound dangerous," Kearn said as we watched a blue and white cop car turn the corner from Fullerton onto the Parkway.

Just before the cops entered the building, Scott said, "I didn't like him, but he didn't deserve to die."

Of course, we were questioned. When we mentioned the phone calls, connections were quickly made to the bombing. Kearn used his cell phone to call the station with the news. He also said he'd check his source to see if he knew any more.

While he called, Jantoro, the detective, showed up. After he questioned us, I asked, "Had he talked to the police about the bombing?"

"All I know is that he was in the deli, and he gave them the news about a woman named Susan Clancey."

"How is she connected to the explosion?"

"I don't know. He was pretty vague about how he found out about her visit."

"He knew everybody in town who was any kind of activist. He has for years. Did he mention anything about the videotapes of the rescue efforts?"

"Not that I heard."

"He said something about them in the message he left us. Can we find the person who knew they were taking him down and ask why?"

"Maybe," Jantoro said. "What was the deal with the videotapes?"

"I don't know. He could have been being mysterious or he could have known something."

Jantoro said, "All the television stations voluntarily gave their tapes to the police. People have been going over them for several days. Nobody reported anything suspicious. I'll have to give them a call."

"Maybe he was overdramatizing his role," Scott suggested. "He did that a lot, or maybe he just wanted to be on television."

"He had a big ego," I said, "but he wouldn't lie."

Kearn rejoined us. "I found a second source on the Clancey rumor. Did you know she was at a convention in Madison last weekend? Not too far to drive down for the afternoon."

Jantoro said, "We'll contact the organizers to see if she was actually present the entire time."

"Myrtle Mae had dinner at Fattatuchi's Deli," Scott said, "but the first time we talked he told me he didn't know anything."

I said, "Maybe it was one of those deals where he didn't know that he knew something. Or he saw something that cost him his life."

"Or it was random urban violence," Scott said. "Or a relative who wanted to inherit his money."

"Which are also possible," I said. "He had a companion of sorts, a John Werner."

"We'll try to contact him," Jantoro said.

I used Scott's cell phone to call the operator to get Werner's number. He didn't answer.

Interviews finished, for several minutes we watched nothing happen outside of Myrtle Mae's building. The guard from McCutcheon's firm, a man with a goatee, stood next to our car, which was illegally parked fifty feet away.

Scott asked, "Are you okay? You've been friends a long time."

"I'll miss his humor. His imitations of both Mayor Daleys were classic bits of humor. His impersonation of Republicans in the U.S. House was beyond hysterical."

Myrtle Mae's death was another emotional bombshell that added to my sense of physical disorientation. I needed time to sort out the horrors that had happened, but I didn't feel I had that luxury at that moment.

I asked Kearn, "Could we get access to the videotapes from the scene of the explosion?"

"Sure, but I was planning to talk to Lyle Gibson, the leader of the protesters. He's finally agreed to an interview. He's insisted it be off camera. Do you two want to come along? We can get the tapes afterward if you want."

I eagerly accepted. "On the way I'd like to check on John Werner."

There was no answer at his condo across from North Pier. The doorman said he'd gone out several hours before.

◣ 22 ◢

Scott and I drove with Kearn. Our guard followed us in his car.

I said, "We have two names of protesters who might be dangerous, Edward Eggleston and Omega Collins."

"I've got their names in a list of the protesters. What did you find out about them?"

I told him. When I finished, Kearn said, "I'll put their names on the top of the list to interview."

We were on the Dan Ryan Expressway going south. I said, "I've heard about Gibson, but I've never met him."

"You must have seen him outside the clinic."

"I always entered by the back way."

"Big, bald fella. He always dresses in black, head to toe. He called a press conference earlier today. He claimed he was in mourning for the children who died in the explosion. He has a congregation in Park Forest in the south suburbs. I've been looking up his background. We've got a big file on him at the station. He worked hard at making sure his was an integrated church years before the demographics of his congregation began to change."

"How'd he get involved in the protests?"

"It seems to have been a gradual thing. His parents were in mainstream Protestant religions. Gibson attended several theology schools. Nothing enormously radical in any of them. How or why he changed to radicalism is unclear. Besides leading the protests, he's opened his home to the itinerant demonstrators on the traveling antiabortion circuit."

"Would he harbor a killer?"

"That has never been proven. Several years ago a suspect in one of the earlier clinic killings was reported in the Chicago area. I would find it hard to believe that the killer was being hidden in Chicago and not have contact with Gibson."

"It sounds like these itinerant protesters leach off the poor and ignorant."

"There's a long history of kindness to travelers in the true Christian tradition. The movement isn't fueled by a lot of money. These folks help each other. In a lot of ways it's very communal in a sort of sixties, hippie way."

I said, "I guess you gotta get your communal experience where you can."

Scott said, "Communal living and a hippie lifestyle always struck me as being about peace, gentleness, and the summer of love."

Kearn said, "Many of these folks are looking for a quiet and peaceful life, a simpler life."

I said, "Except the ones who write fraudulent checks and blow other people up."

"I've interviewed some of them. They aren't inherently evil. At least the ones who aren't trying to get their faces on the cameras. I think it's too simple to dismiss them as right-wing dupes."

I said, "Especially not if they're determined to blow up the rest of us. It sounds like you've got some sympathy for them."

"I've got sympathy for people who believe sincerely and aren't out for themselves. The phony ones are usually obvious. Unfortunately, when they're on camera, the station won't let us put captions under their names like 'hypocritical preacher' or 'publicity-hungry nut.' "

"Is that what Gibson is like?"

"I'll let you judge for yourself. I'll tell you this much. He ran for the Illinois House a few years ago. He ran an immaculately clean campaign. Every penny was scrupulously accounted for. He got clobbered in the primary, but at least he was honest."

"I'll save my sainthood medal for him until after I've met him."

Scott said, "Do terrorists and heaven mix? A few of these antiabortion people do have a lot in common with the militia people."

"I don't understand that at all," I said. "I can't think of more disparate groups."

"I disagree," Scott said. "They want the government out of their lives except when they want it to interfere in people's lives when somebody makes a decision they don't like. A lot of these folks are from rural areas, but you better not take away their farm subsidies."

I asked, "Isn't he going to be surprised when three of us show up on his doorstep?"

"Yeah," Kearn said. "I doubt if he's going to confess anything to me. If he was planning that, he'd invite the entire press corps to make sure he made a colossal splash. I figure with you guys, it might get him a little off-balance. If so, maybe I'll get something significant. I realize I'm most likely

191

to get a lot of self-righteous ranting from the guy. So far I've got nothing. I'm beginning to think this assignment is useless. I'm not going to catch an international terrorist. As long as it boosts the ratings, we'll keep covering it."

We exited Interstate 57 at U.S. 30. We drove past Lincoln Mall and the strip of stores between it and the Metra Tracks, which I always thought of as the dividing line between Matteson and Park Forest. We made a right on Orchard Drive, drove three blocks, and turned left. I watched for the house number as Kearn drove. We pulled up in front of a modest-sized ranch home on the south side of the street.

Gibson answered the door himself. He was medium height with an immense full beard and bristly hair in a haystack halo around half of his head. He gave a cheerful smile and held out his hand to Kearn. "I recognize you from the news." He peered at Scott and me. "Your faces look a little familiar. Aren't you the baseball player and his lover?" He reached out and shook our hands. So much for discomfort leading to some kind of chink in his armor. He invited us in. His voice boomed. He welcomed us profusely, offered to give us a tour. We declined. He insisted on getting us something to drink. We trooped into a spotless kitchen. I asked for water. Kearn and Scott got generic-brand, orange soft drinks. Three kids all under the age of five rushed through the kitchen into a family room beyond. They clasped hands, twirled for a few moments in a circle, then fell in a giggling heap on the ground. Gibson set his generic-brand, grape soft drink down on a high shelf and joined the kids on the floor. He listened to them carefully explain what it was they were about. He then directed their activity to a set of blocks and trains, which they fell to with alacrity. He retrieved his drink and sat down on a rust-colored ottoman. We sat on matching sofa sectional pieces.

"What can I do for you?" he asked brightly.

If the man was any more cheerful, he might become a menace to a free society.

"I'm a little uncomfortable discussing what we have to in front of the children," Kearn said.

"Nothing you can say will hurt them," Gibson said. "They understand the Lord's business."

"We want to talk about the killings at the clinic," Kearn said.

"A tragic thing," Gibson said.

The lack of compassion in his voice irritated me. How could he seem so cheerful? I'd certainly been in the presence of people who hated me passionately. I'd learned some degree of calm, but I felt free to say, "I was in the explosion."

"I'm sorry." But still cheerful. "I know you imagine we had something to do with the explosion, but let me assure you, violence is counterproductive to our efforts. Some people who are upset at the murder of the unborn have committed deplorable acts. I don't agree with them, but I understand their anger and their frustration."

"But you don't seem upset by what happened."

"The people who died are with Jesus. If I were called in the next minute, I know my soul would be ready to meet my maker. I don't know about their immortal souls, but I always hope for the best."

"You had a whole banquet full of possible terrorists in town," I said. "Any one of them could have done it."

"And the police have interviewed them. None of the people I know believe in violence. You know the obvious answer. If they were at the banquet, they couldn't have set the bomb."

I said, "Maybe that's why God invented timing devices."

"Do you know all of the people who were at the banquet?"

Scott asked. "Can you vouch that they are all incapable of violence?"

"You know no one could possibly vouch for every single one. Do you really think that's a sensible question?"

Kearn asked, "Did you know Susan Clancey was supposed to be in town?"

Gibson's smile completely disappeared. "If we would have known she was planning to be in Chicago, we would certainly have made sure it was splashed all over the papers. She has committed mass murder. She will be punished. If not here, then in a life in hell in the hereafter."

Now he was sounding like a fundamentalist minister preaching hate instead of Christianity. In an odd way I found that comforting. The enemy was exactly what I thought him to be. Few things clear the mind like an obvious enemy acting in a way that fits all the prejudices. Very much like a school administrator acting like a moronic twit, which would be a cliché if it weren't so true.

Gibson breathed deeply for several moments. Then his smile began to return. "But I'm sure I would have heard if she was coming to town."

"Do any of your protesters have any expertise in explosives?" Kearn asked.

"You know the police asked these questions already. I wonder why you're here. A reporter and two national spokespersons for the gay agenda."

"I'm here doing some follow-up on the explosion," Kearn said. "Obviously you and your group form a significant part of the story. You've been out there for years protesting."

"Rain or shine. Heat or cold."

"I'm here," I said, "because I've been personally threatened. Friends of mine died in the explosion."

"Doing a little investigating on your own? Hoping the evil

leader of the pro-life crowd will confess to you the error of his ways?" Gibson gave an uproarious laugh. The children looked at him briefly, then returned to their play.

Gibson said, "I abhor violence. The next time I am arrested, it will be my one hundredth time. Not one of the arrests was for a violent act. I did not plant the bomb. I know nothing about explosives."

"But there are some in the movement who have done violence," Kearn said. "There are dead doctors here and in Canada."

"People take their chances when they take the lives of children. We are believers, but because we believe does not inherently make us violent. Belief is a valid concept."

"What is the nature of belief?" Scott asked. "Isn't that the basic question?"

"Perhaps," Gibson said.

I wasn't sure there was much point in engaging Gibson in a theological or philosophical debate. Scott thinks debate and reason will lead to truth. I have my doubts.

"And isn't belief itself a choice?" Scott asked. "And isn't what one believes a choice?"

"Not according to the church," Gibson said.

"But when you say according to the church, haven't you let them do your thinking for you? You've abandoned your own identity to that of a collective mind that has been proven wrong. Look at all the torture and murder that have happened and continue to happen in the name of God."

"Evil exists in the world. You cannot blame God for that."

Scott said, "What I don't get is, how you can abandon logic and reason and switch to God and belief? Why do people of faith prefer abstract thought over empirical observation?"

"But don't you believe in all kinds of things that you cannot see? When you turn on a light, do you 'believe' in electricity? Do you discuss its nature and origins or do you trust those who invented it? It works. It is the same thing with faith. Because you don't know how it runs doesn't mean it does not exist. I do not understand the laws of physics, but planes still stay in the air."

Scott said, "I don't see the validity of equating observable physical phenomena with the existence of a god."

"I can see God's plan in the fall of a sparrow. God is in everything. You make the mistake of enshrining reason and logic above all else. The world doesn't run on logic and reason. There's an awful lot of emotion and feeling, belief and faith. Reason and logic are not enough."

Scott said, "I find that reason and logic are all there is. If you abandon reason and logic, you're left with little more than voodoo."

"But I can deny your basic premises as easily as you can deny mine."

Kearn interrupted, "Fascinating as all this is, I was wondering if you knew how we could get in touch with Omega Collins or Edward Eggleston."

"For what purpose?"

"To interview them as we have you. Because I have a source who says they are the ones in your organization who are most likely to be prone to violence. Do you know if they have the expertise to build a bomb?"

"Expertise to build a bomb? That's no criterion for suspicion in this day and age. All you need is a computer hooked up to the Internet. You yourself must have thought of the Internet connection. Pish, tosh."

I hadn't heard the old-fashioned dismissive since I was a child listening to my grandmother.

Gibson continued, "Everyone knows about the theory that there was a secret terrorist cell in the building across the alley from the clinic. I doubt if the bombing had anything to do with my group. Shouldn't you be investigating these terrorists?"

One of the children crawled into his lap and snuggled against his massive bulk. She leaned her head against his neck and closed her eyes. He cradled her gently.

"If the police questioned them," Kearn said, "why would it hurt if I talked to them?"

"If my friends were inclined to confess, and I'm not saying they have anything to confess, why would they pick you and not their priest? For that matter, why you and not the police?"

"I prefer to talk to sources directly," Kearn said.

"Very sensible," Gibson conceded.

"It will simply be a matter of time before I find them independently," Kearn said. "Why not help us?"

"Honestly, many of the people in the movement don't have permanent addresses. They come to town and those of us who live here open our houses and our pocketbooks to them."

Even though I understood it, his unwillingness to help irritated me. Truculence began to erode my veneer of calm. I said, "They sound like a bunch of freeloaders who've learned how to get a meal ticket from poor saps who they've duped."

"I prefer to call it the triumph of Christianity rather than the victory of cynicism. I won't help you find my people. Many of them will be leaving now anyway. There is nothing more to protest at that clinic. There is nothing to hold them here."

"Convenient for you," I said.

"I understand how you feel. It must have been awful being in the explosion."

"I don't think you do understand how I feel. You've been on the giving-out side of the protests. How can you possibly know what living on the other side of fear feels like?"

"You made your choices." The fatuous smile plastered on his face as he said this really pissed me off.

Before my anger could burst out into a less than helpful tirade, Kearn stood up and said, "Thank you for your time, Mr. Gibson."

Gibson adjusted the child in his arms and got to his feet. "If any of you ever feel the need to have a further philosophical or theological discussion, please come by. I'd be happy to chat as long as you like. I've been accused of everything already, so you can be as angry as you like, but if you want to get down to the nature of belief and the existence of God or anything else, I'd be happy to talk. I'm here for you."

I hate it when somebody says "I'm here for you" and he or she isn't being sarcastic. I'm afraid he was deadly serious. "What I need," I said, "is for reason and logic to triumph."

We left.

Outside, Kearn said, "I've never actually heard someone have that lengthy of a calm debate with him. How did you do it?"

Scott said, "I was fascinated. Here was this guy in his native habitat. I wanted to hear him."

"To what end?" I asked.

"Because I was willing to listen to him," Scott said, "didn't mean I agreed with him."

I said, "I didn't like him."

"I can understand you not liking him because you presume he's homophobic," Kearn said.

"That's part of it," I said. "What I hated most was that smile. I've seen that same fatuous grin on Phyllis Schlafly's face, Bob Bennett's, George Will's, Jerry Falwell's, all those right-wing talking heads. That smile that says something like, 'You poor child, how quaint that you want to take part in the adult world. I will tolerate your silly prattle for a few moments, but we all really know that what you have to say is nonsense and not worth my time.' "

"All that from a smile?" Kearn asked.

"And more," I said. "Look at those pursed lips of George Will's. They make him look as if he were permanently in charge of changing society's diapers."

As Kearn started the car, he said, "I'd love to get you guys and Gibson on the same talk show. You'd set ratings records."

Scott said, "We'd bore each other and the audience to death."

Kearn said, "You've thought about the nature of belief and your relationship to the world. Thoughtful men are in short supply." He pointed to Scott in the backseat. "Where the hell did you learn all that?"

I know how Scott hates to be denigrated by people who think he's stupid simply because he's a jock. However, he replied mildly, "I applied some simple logic to his basic beliefs. He's right that logic doesn't run the world. I just wish it did more often."

Kearn said, "Take it that I'm making you an official offer for an interview anytime it is convenient for you and your lover, or you and any combination of people I can get my bosses to agree to."

Scott murmured a noncommittal, "We'll have to see."

"I'd really like to do some groundwork for a story connected with you guys. None of the other reporters have been able to get past your agent or your answering service. I've been helpful. What do you think about some payback?"

Scott said, "We don't know if we're part of the solution. And we don't know if anything we do might set someone off or cause ourselves more danger or more hassle."

Kearn sighed. "Okay. But I get an exclusive if there's a story to be found here."

We agreed on that.

Kearn said, "If you guys don't have anything planned at the moment, I've got time to assemble those tapes from the night of the explosion. I'd like to view them with you."

He was doing us a favor so I could hardly say, "I'd rather not have you there."

We tried John Werner's home phone, but got no answer. We stopped by, but the doorman again said he had gone out earlier and not returned.

Back at the television station, Kearn found copies of the tapes. We brought them back to our penthouse. Kearn gazed at the view, then he stopped, as most visitors do, at Scott's trophy table. We keep his high school state baseball trophy on the table with his Major League Most Valuable Player and Cy Young awards. "Very nice," Kearn murmured. When he finished his observations, we took the tapes to the electronics center. This was an interior room with four mismatched, deliciously comfortable easy chairs, surrounded by state-of-the-art electronic everything. "You want to see all of these?" he asked. "They go on for nearly forty hours. It's everything all the crews got."

"I'd like to go over anything you've got connected to me from that night," Scott said. "Whoever was stalking me might have been caught in a shot. Let's start there."

I added, "We should also look through all of it. Maybe

we'll see people who look out of place to us, or maybe we'll recognize someone."

Kearn inserted a tape. It showed a group of surly-looking men with TEAMSTERS ON STRIKE signs gathered around a priest kneeling on the ground.

"What was that?" I asked.

Kearn pressed the fast-forward button. "The story we were on just before the bombing. A priest knew the leaders of both sides of the strike. He was trying to mediate the solution. He got a nasty club on the head for his troubles."

"Hard for me to picture a priest as a Teamster," I said.

Unedited tape can make for remarkably intense viewing. Or as is more likely, be intensely boring, filled with inarticulate people or mistakes or dead time while film continues to run. In the first few minutes we saw Kearn in high-speed jerks begin an interview four times. Then a lot of Teamsters milling around. Then several minutes of postmelee interview shots from the strike. A few seconds of transition tape passed by. The bombing coverage began with a swaying and jiggling camera moving rapidly toward the block where the clinic had been. There was nothing boring about the fire scene. I hadn't viewed any of the coverage on television. I was entranced.

They hadn't caught my actual rescue. The cameras had extensive coverage of Alan Redpath. We ran the first tape straight through. We spent another hour on it, going backward and forward, pausing numerous times so Scott and I could examine different faces, postures, walks, body structure. They had caught about ten minutes total of Scott and the people around him. Nothing gave us any hint of possible attackers or clues to who may have caused the explosion.

After the third hour, I asked, "Can we keep all these and watch the rest of them later? I'm a little tired." I wanted Kearn to leave and couldn't think of a polite way to tell him to go home.

"They're copies," Kearn said. "I'd rather you didn't let them out of your hands, but you can keep them for now. I'm certainly building up points here for a possible interview."

"Yeah, you are," I agreed. He left.

After he was gone, I sat for half an hour, remote control in hand, and inspected the tapes. I couldn't figure out what it was Myrtle Mae had seen that he wanted to tell us about.

I found Scott rummaging in the freezer for some ice cream when the phone rang. It was John Werner.

"Have you heard about . . . ," I began.

"Yes." John sounded awful. "I could use some company."

I'd known John almost as long as I had Myrtle Mae. I told him we'd be right over.

I said to Scott, "I'm beat, but it's only just nine o'clock. Let's go see Werner."

Scott said, "I'm sure it won't take long for the security guard to get here."

I was annoyed at how rapidly Scott always thought of calling the security firm, but he's nothing if not consistent. Only Greg Maddox in baseball can put a pitch where he wants it more dependably than Scott. If consistency were a virtue, Scott would be a saint. Of course, if being a slob was a virtue, I'd be a saint. You gotta go with your strengths.

The guard picked us up in ten minutes. Werner lived on Fullerton between Clark and Halsted. There is no parking in that part of town unless you have one of the neighborhood stickers. We finally found a spot in the minuscule Tower Records lot on Beldon and walked over.

Werner's home was furnished much like Myrtle Mae's. A few simple but solid antiques. He and I hugged as we entered the house. He looked as if he'd been crying. We sat near the picture window looking out onto Fullerton. The trees outside had almost completely lost their leaves.

"I can't believe he's dead. I never knew anyone so vibrant. We'd known each other for over fifty years. Longer than I knew anyone except my parents and my brother. That's a long time."

"Were you ever lovers?" Scott asked.

"Never lovers, not really, but we've been dear friends for years. He and I had brunch at the Drake Hotel every Sunday since before the dinosaurs." John sighed. "We met in high school. We were each other's first sexual partners. We were both from Watseka, Illinois. If the cornfields could have talked our senior year of high school, what tales they would have to tell. We weren't run out of town, not literally, but we both fled together."

"I heard he ran away from home," I said.

"Numerous times, but his family spent a great deal of money to get him back. He was a rebel from the first I knew him. He was gorgeous back then. Not as effeminate as he put on later, although he was always a little nellie, but he was very pretty. A heartbreaker."

I asked, "Did he really have all those strange jobs I heard about?"

Werner smiled. "All those and more. He was always willing to take a risk. He was a window washer on high-rise apartment houses. He worked maintenance for a few months on the Golden Gate Bridge."

I said, "I don't remember him having much qualification for any of the jobs I heard about."

"A lot of them didn't require a lot of skill, but if they did, it didn't bother him. He would lie if he had to. It was even

203

better if the job irritated his family. Sometimes the two motivations became pretty entangled. You know he was in the service during the Korean War?"

"He never mentioned it."

"He always claimed it was in one of those highly secretive branches of the service, some kind of special intelligence unit. He'd always laugh and say if he told me, he'd have to kill me. I never took it seriously."

"Is the world ready for James Bond disguised as a drag queen?" I asked.

Werner smiled slightly. "He claimed the most daring thing he ever did to defy his parents was to join a Trappist monastery."

"Why was that so terrible?" Scott asked.

"His family were rock-ribbed, fundamentalist Protestants at a time when and a place where that meant intense hatred for Catholics and the pope. That's when they cut him off for good. For over forty years he had no contact with his family."

I thought of the positive relationship I have with my family and the complications we've encountered with Scott's. Compared to Myrtle Mae, we were fairly lucky.

"All those strange jobs were actually very necessary. He had to eat. But even in the most macho of jobs, he was always himself. He was never phony. He also never lasted long in any of them. He just wouldn't compromise. He had an awful tough exterior. He had to have, but inside he was always a sweetheart, a pussycat, a gentle soul." John used a tissue to wipe his eyes. "Who would kill him?"

"We want to know that too."

"The police talked to me. They wanted to know where I was this morning. I spend one day a week volunteering at the Harold Washington Library as a guide. I have everyone who was on a tour today as a witness."

204

"Had he had any major fights with anyone?" I asked.

"I have no clue. He's done a lot of activist things over the years that I thought were risky. I warned him over and over again about taking public stands, but he said someone had to do it. I always asked why he had to be the one making statements to the media and being so visible. He made politicians uncomfortable, but he didn't care. He was tough. I understand how valuable it is to take a stand, but not to get killed over it."

"He and I worked for a lot of the same gay rights causes," I said, "but that's seldom lethal. There might be a stinging barb on a talk show, but nothing really deadly."

Scott said, "He claimed he ate at the Fattatuchis' deli quite often. Is that true?"

"Yes. Thank God he got out in time. Mostly he stayed in of an evening. He was on medicine for high blood pressure and had pills to help lower his cholesterol. He had all the health problems associated with getting older and being a great deal overweight."

"He never mentioned that," I said.

"He wouldn't. He didn't sleep much anymore. He stayed home and was addicted to overnight news shows. He taped every program that had any connection with gay people." Again John dabbed at his eyes. "He was just trying to make the world a little better place and somebody killed him."

I said, "He left us a message about the overnight news. We didn't know what it meant."

"He left me one as well." Werner tapped the play button on his answering machine. Myrtle Mae's voice came on: "John, did you watch the late news overnight? The coverage of the bombing? I've got to get a copy of that. You never watch the news. I've got to make some calls. I think I'm onto something."

205

"Do you know what that meant?" Werner asked.

"We got the same kind of message. We don't know either."

Werner knew absolutely nothing that would help us find Myrtle Mae's killer. We stayed and offered him sympathy for as long as was comfortable. On the way home I felt miserably depressed. I would miss Myrtle Mae.

Scott prowled around the apartment cleaning. While he is a neatnick almost to a fault, and I am a slob to a fault, he usually confines his cleaning binges to particular times of the day and week. For half an hour I tried to read myself to sleep with indifferent success. I found him scrubbing one of the guest bathrooms.

"Problem?" I asked. "You usually don't clean at nearly midnight."

"I'm not sleepy."

"Are you okay?"

"Just worried about us and danger, and I keep thinking about the scene of the explosion and how close I came to losing you. I'm afraid I've begun to worry as much as you do."

"And that's bad?"

"You're so good at worrying for both of us."

I let it go at his light comment. Something was bugging him, but whatever it was would take time to emerge. I'd sensed it at the hospital. I wished he would just tell me. I didn't have the energy or desire to push him just then.

I held him close. He put the cleansers and disinfectant away, and we went to bed and cuddled briefly. I felt great comfort in his closeness as I always do, but that good feeling didn't help me get to sleep. I too remembered the scene and how close my own death had come. I lay awake far into the night trying to shut down my mind.

▴ 23 ▴

The next morning Angus Thieme's terrorism contact, Owen Harvey, paged us through the answering service. We returned his call immediately.

"I've got an address for Omega Collins. If you want to talk to her, you might give it a try."

"Has she been named as a suspect?" I asked.

"The police have questioned her several times. I don't know how significant that is. I can't go myself. There's a threat in Iraq again. Nothing will come of it, but I've got to go. I tried to call Brandon Kearn to follow this up, but I couldn't get hold of him this morning."

"He didn't answer his pager?"

"Nope. I gotta go. My plane leaves in fifty minutes, and I need to find a cab that can get me to O'Hare on time."

I thanked him for the tip.

I tried calling Kearn but had no luck. We decided to go see her ourselves. We got our security person and drove over. Omega was staying just across the border from Chicago in Cicero. We knocked on the door on the south side of a duplex that looked as if it would need teams of builders working for years to get it in livable shape. When we knocked, a tall, skinny teenager with ghastly acne answered the door. I had never seen larger zits on a human being, and that's saying a lot from someone who teaches high school. I felt sorry for him.

We asked for Omega. His voice squeaked as he called over his shoulder, "Ma, more visitors."

A woman, thin to the point of emaciation, strode toward us from the interior of the house. She gave us a half smile. She wore a flower-print dress that drooped on her frame. Her skin seemed more gray than pink. Her hair hung to just below her ears as if a large bowl had been hung over her and someone had lopped off all the sides leaving a small space for her facial features.

We introduced ourselves.

"Lyle Gibson said you'd been to see him. He thought you'd find out where I was staying. Although, he said there would be three of you. Would you like to come in?"

We entered. The hardwood floors creaked loudly. Any stain, varnish, or wax had long since worn off them. She led us into a room that was furnished with only simple straight-back chairs. She made no apology or comment about the home or the furnishings. A cross with a grotesquely suffering Christ hung on one wall. The other had a picture of Christ with a glowing red heart on top of his chest and a golden halo surrounding his head.

We sat down. She folded her hands in her lap and gave us a slight smile. "Gentlemen?"

I said, "I know we aren't the police, but we'd like to ask you a few questions."

"It doesn't matter to me if you are police or reporters or

lost souls. I am at peace. You may ask whatever you will."

"Did you blow up the Human Services Clinic?" I asked.

"No."

"Did you have any part in the bombing at all?"

"No. I don't believe in violence."

"You know that violence happens at all the clinics you protest at."

"Violence happens when people try to kill children. I am not the cause of it. I don't begin it. I don't believe in it. Jesus brought a message of love."

Her voice sounded like a computer-enhanced tin whistle. I was horrified at the lack of emotion.

Scott began a biblical discussion that sounded like a repeat of the one we had with the Reverend Mr. Gibson. Useless as I thought it was, I didn't stop him. They both spoke softly but dogmatically. I'd rather have anvils dropped on my head than listen to the two of them. When a significant pause for mutual respect occurred, I asked, "Do you know where Mr. Eggleston is?"

"He left town the day after the explosion. I believe he's organizing some demonstrations in Seattle."

"Why wouldn't Gibson tell us that?"

"You'd have to ask him." She knew nothing or was unwilling to tell us anything helpful about the bombing.

Out in the car Scott said, "That was unsettling."

"How so?"

"I wish these people would rant and spew hatred. It would make it a lot easier to hate them back."

"Life can be ambiguous like that."

At home the answering service had a message from Gloria Dellios. She wanted to meet us at her apartment. It was getting totally annoying by this time waiting for a security guard to show up before we could go anyplace. I'm not sure what real good they did. Anybody with a high-powered rifle a couple hundred yards away could probably kill us both in a matter of seconds before any guard could react. I figured it wasn't time to start that argument again.

Gloria Dellios opened her apartment door. She looked as pale and drawn as the last time we'd met. Another woman was in the room. Dellios introduced us to Susan Clancey, the late-term-abortion doctor.

Susan Clancey was what used to be called a full-figured woman. Her imposing heft was augmented by her being nearly six feet tall. With her silver spectacles and gray hair cut in soft feathers, she could have been anybody's grand-mother.

After we were seated, Clancey began, "We wanted to find out what the police know. Gloria thought you might have a contact with the police, the press, or both who were working on the case." Her voice was pleasantly modulated.

Scott said, "Everyone's been looking for you."

"We know. I'm not sure what to do."

"You're not a suspect," I said. "It's your coming to town that might have made a difference. If people knew about it, then it could be significant."

"I'm afraid I let it slip while I was in Madison. Several members of the right wing had infiltrated the convention."

"Do you know who?"

"No."

"Why not tell this to the police?"

"I want to, but I want to do it carefully. I don't want more controversy attached to my name."

"Is that realistic?" I asked. "Won't you be controversial wherever you go for the rest of your life?"

210

"I don't really think someone would bomb that whole area to kill one person. That doesn't make sense. I may be an object of hatred, but if you've got the expertise to make a bomb, you've got the wherewithal to buy a high-powered rifle and take a shot at me."

Dellios said, "Another problem is that the clinic owners have expressly forbidden us to perform the late-term procedures. They were afraid of even more protests and negative publicity. I arranged for Dr. Clancey to come to town on my own. My sister needed the procedure done. She's had a lot of medical complications with the latest pregnancy. She will probably die without the procedure." Dellios's voice trailed off as she finished, "She has enough kids already."

"I was not aware of those rules," Clancey said. "I came to town in good faith."

"Why did you want to see us?" Scott asked.

"If people think I was at the clinic, they may blame me for getting all those people killed. The right-wing crazies will claim it's my fault for coming to town."

I said, "You know what they say is ludicrous. Why give credence to their raving?"

"It's perception as much as anything. And I was there. Gloria and I left together. I haven't told anyone that I was part of the explosion."

"Why not?"

Dellios said, "I received a bomb threat minutes after Susan arrived."

"You knew and you didn't order an evacuation?" I found it hard to breathe. I tried to stand up, but found myself dizzier than when I'd woke up in the hospital. In seconds Scott was at my side and helping me to sit back down.

Dellios said, "You must understand, we get hundreds of those kinds of calls a year. The call came directly into my

211

private line. I figured someone was using it for harassment purposes. We have those metal detectors. We inspect all packages and purses. No one could bring anything in. I didn't expect something like this. How could anyone?"

"How would you know what to expect?" I asked. "This is criminally negligent."

"It seemed like just another threat. I thought of simply logging it in with the others. I decided to get Susan out of the building. I thought about her first."

"We're lovers," Clancey said. "When I discovered that she got me out to keep me safe, I was angry as well. I was the one who insisted we go back in and warn everyone. We were on our way when the explosion occurred. The delay was less than five minutes."

"I killed all those people." Dellios buried her head in Clancey's bosom and wept.

It took nearly ten minutes for everyone's emotions to calm down enough to continue any kind of discussion. I asked, "You're a doctor, why didn't you stay to help?"

"Gloria was screened somewhat. I wasn't. I landed on my head and shoulder. I had a concussion. I was in a hospital myself until this morning."

"Gloria better get herself a lawyer," I said. "She's going to need one."

"I'm not liable. I didn't plant the bomb."

"You'd both better come forward," I said.

"Did the caller mention anything that would help the police?" Scott asked.

"All I can say is that it was a male. Not a kid, but that's all I know."

We left them without learning anything helpful in finding out who did the bombing.

On the way to the car Scott asked, "You really think they could arrest Gloria Dellios?"

"Five minutes could have saved a lot of lives."

In the car McCutcheon said, "There was just a special bulletin on the radio. Braxton Thornburg died in the explosion."

"The Internet rumor was true?" I asked.

"Must have been."

Scott asked, "What was he doing in Chicago?"

"Hiding in those old buildings across the alley from the clinic. You can talk about being a survivalist in the wilderness, but when it comes right down to it, getting swallowed up in the middle of a large city is probably more effective. The report said he'd cut his hair short and dyed it blond. He no longer had a beard and had lost fifty pounds."

"So the conspiracy theorists are right again," Scott said. "There really was a terrorist cell of sorts nearby."

"It was only one guy," McCutcheon said.

"Do they think he did the bombing?" I asked.

"The news report didn't say. They certainly must be concentrating on him."

We stopped to see Alan Redpath. His bed was surrounded with cheery balloons and smiling stuffed animals. The poor kid was in the same position we'd seen him last. The machines showed life. I saw the tiny chest rise and fall. Alvana's brother nodded and smiled at us. The doctors still weren't sure if Alan would live. I stepped next to the bed. I touched the little boy's hair and patted his face. If I believed in prayer, now was when I would utter one.

24

In the elevator at the penthouse I said, "I'm going to call all of our sources. We should get all of them together."

"Won't that piss some of them off?" Scott asked.

"If we got everybody together, maybe we could coordinate efforts. If we pooled information, we might get somewhere or at least get nowhere a lot faster. It would save a lot of driving around aimlessly."

"And if we piss some of them off, then we won't get any help. Some of these people agreed to help us if we were the only ones who know about it."

I said, "I think the only one who might be chancy is the detective, Pulver. The rest of them are journalists. I think we should call Borini and Faslo as well. If we get the whole aggregation together, maybe we'll get something."

"I doubt it."

"I'm willing to listen to other suggestions."

"I'm willing to listen to all kinds of suggestions, I just don't happen to think this is a very good one."

"So stay away from the meeting."

"If they even all decide to show up."

"We could just not tell any of them we were inviting the others."

"Are you listening to yourself? Do you think this is making sense?"

Inside the penthouse Scott paced the living room. He seemed unable to sit down. I stood with my back against the unlit fireplace and waited. When he's restless, it means he wants to talk. I guessed calling our sources wasn't a great idea, but it was all I had at the moment.

Scott abruptly stopped moving and said, "I am such a screwup. Everything I did before you woke up has been a disaster. I lost my cool, that was the problem. If I'd been as calm as I should have been, I'd have thought longer."

"Aren't you being a little tough on yourself? At least you tried to do something. Not like Gloria Dellios when she got the bomb threat."

He exploded, "How can you get a bomb threat and not evacuate the building? That is madness. How can anybody be involved in that type of thing? And Myrtle Mae thinking he knew something. He probably didn't. It was probably another one of his hysterical overreactions to a misinterpretation of data. Maybe it killed him. And now you want to call all our sources together. Have you thought about the implications of that? We've barely discussed it."

"What's to discuss?"

"You need to put more thought into what you do. Like with the clinic. You're lucky your name wasn't on one of those Internet lists of people working at such places."

"I was just a volunteer. I was never paid. No one really knew."

"What difference does that make? It was dangerous. What

kind of friend asks you to come to work at such a dangerous place?"

"I beg your pardon."

"Look what's happened all because you can't pass up the chance to make a statement or help a cause. Somebody's got a grievance, you're there with a picket sign. I don't care about your goddamn causes."

"Aren't you the famous openly gay baseball player, the focal point of a major cause?"

"It's not the same. That's personal and directly effects our well-being. With you, everything that comes along, you're committed to."

"Not everything."

"Too much, too often. And look where it's put you."

"The victims are responsible for being attacked? I don't think so. And you don't believe that either. You've always supported my working in causes before."

"It hasn't gotten you nearly killed."

"You're really angry."

"Don't do that psychobabble crap to me. I don't need my feelings named, repeated, or analyzed. I know I'm totally pissed."

It drives me nuts when something he's been holding back turns into an explosion. I wish he could tell me before he erupts. I know it is hard to just be open. Nevertheless, I was irritated. "Why couldn't you talk about this earlier?"

"Right, in the hospital? You'd just woken up from being unconscious. I'm not sure I could have articulated what I was worried about or angry about. How come you're so goddamn sure if everyone just told the truth everything would be fine? Nobody, including you, indulges in instant truth every time a thought or a feeling strikes them. I was petrified of losing you."

"I've been fine for several days."

"Don't you pull that sanctimonious crap with me."

"You get to determine what my reactions are?"

"That's not what I meant. You know it takes me time to articulate my feelings. I'm doing my best. Right now I'm saying I'm scared. This whole situation is out of control. We run from one useless interview to another. I don't think we should take any more risks. I think we should just drop this."

"You think you're the only one allowed to take risks? We don't ask each other for permission."

"But we discuss things. You don't just call up every contact in an investigation and call them here. You've got to think about it. Plan it."

"How is calling them all here that awful? How could that increase the danger?"

"If one of them's a killer, it could be lethal."

"They don't run around toting bombs. And any one of them could have pulled a gun and shot both of us at some point in the last few days. Friends of mine died in that explosion. Alvana's child is still not out of danger."

"Look, I'm too upset to discuss this more right now. If I keep talking, I'll just want to inflict hurt. I don't want to do that. I want to still talk about all this, but I need to take a break. I'll be back in a little while."

I stood silently in front of the windows. He grabbed his jacket and walked out. We take breaks when we get to an impasse in arguments. We both have big egos and we've learned we need to step back and get perspective.

I brooded as I watched the sunlight on the buildings below. Finding out who the bomber was seemed more unlikely than ever. Discovering who'd been threatening us seemed only slightly more possible. Thinking about it, I decided my idea of setting ourselves out as bait should be tried. When

I'd suggested it to Pulver, I'd gotten shot down. I wanted to put it into operation.

After about twenty minutes, I began to get restless. Scott was outside without his precious guard. I thought I'd at least check the perimeter of the building. When I got to the ground floor, Scott was nowhere in sight. I hung around by the front door for several minutes. I went back upstairs to call McCutcheon. Scott had just phoned in from the western end of Navy Pier, a mile or so from our building. Instead of calling, I figured I'd go meet him. I decided not to try the car. With the often snarled traffic in the area, it would be quicker to walk.

I hurried to find him. I watched as carefully as I could for anyone following me. I assumed Scott had used the path we would normally take when we strolled along the lake. I saw nothing suspicious. I crossed under Lake Shore Drive through the underpass at the northeast corner of the 540 North Lake Shore Drive building.

Two men pushing a baby stroller were my only companions as I hustled through the underpass. I suspected I wasn't taking much of a chance, but my paranoia was beginning to get the best of me.

I emerged in Olive Park. People were out on a bright and pleasant October afternoon. The Ferris wheel in the middle of the pier dominated the view in that direction. Lake Point Towers loomed to my right. I hastened through the park. As I was about to cross the street from the park to the pier itself, I thought I saw Morty Hamilton, Scott's catcher from the team. He was sitting on a bench near the entrance to the pier. He was staring fixedly at the entrance on the south side of the pier. I looked where he was watching. Scott was leaning against the iron fence gazing toward the east.

I began to hurry toward them, but just then Scott moved

away from the gate and began walking toward the east end of the pier. Morty waited a few seconds and began to follow him. He made no move to catch up with Scott. He didn't look back. He moved cautiously as if to avoid being seen.

Suspicion was quickly replaced by certainty. I was furious. I slowed down. As long as no immediate danger threatened, I would wait and watch what the son of a bitch did. Morty had been with the team for little more than a year and a half. Scott had enjoyed hanging around with him on the road. I'd never had cause to think of him as anything but a benign goof. Now, of course, the answer seemed obvious. Here was a link to those who had been threatening Scott.

I lurked twenty-five yards behind Morty. It wasn't hard to keep hidden. He seldom looked around, and sufficiently large crowds of people were around to make quick dashes to cover unnecessary.

We passed several of the cruise ships that took short excursions out onto the lake. One of them gave a loud blast on its horn and pulled away as I moved by.

When Scott got to the end of the pier, he stood there with his head down. The pleasant weather and scenery seemed to hold little interest for him. He looked like a depressed little kid. He shook his head and turned back.

Morty eased himself into a small declivity in the side of the auditorium building that sits at the end of the pier. His only way back was past me. At that moment Scott called out. I looked at him. He'd spotted me. He hurried forward. Morty tried to melt himself into the brick of the building. I rushed toward where he was. Seeing my direction wasn't toward him, Scott hesitated. I pointed. Morty's head swiveled from one to the other of us. His face turned pale.

Scott and I met in front of Morty. "You came after me," Scott said to me.

"I didn't want the one time you left without a guard to be disastrous. I shouldn't have pushed you so hard." We hugged briefly, then turned on Morty.

I said, "He's been following you."

Morty had the grace not to try to lie. "I'm sorry, you guys. I had no choice. I'm sorry. I know it's been bad, but I did everything I could to make things easier."

"What the hell are you talking about?" Scott asked.

Morty sat on one of the benches that looked south toward the Shedd Aquarium and the Adler Planetarium. The harbor in between was already half-empty of boats in preparation for the coming winter. The wind blew softly. People barely glanced at us. Scott was in a baseball cap pulled low over his eyes. This simple disguise was usually enough to keep him from being recognized. While I had been on some talk shows, he'd been on a million of them and had given far more interviews. The commercials he'd done before he came out had made him almost as familiar a figure as Michael Jordan or Jim Palmer.

"You guys gotta understand. It's not my fault." Morty was short and squat in the old-fashioned tradition of baseball catchers. Sitting on the bench, he looked like a dejected bear. "All I did was follow you and report back. I knew it was just supposed to scare you. They weren't gonna really hurt you. They told me I was gonna be sent down to the minor leagues. I had to do this. It was the only way I could keep my career going. They promised me a minor league manager's job. I never even graduated high school. You had everything. I got nothing."

"Who told you all this?"

"A group of the owners decided you were too controversial for baseball. They figured you'd cave under the pressure. They could probably get you out legally, but they didn't want

221

to look like assholes. They hoped nobody would show up for the games when you pitched. They didn't count on the crowds, the goodwill you guys developed, and how tough you both were. Getting me as a spy was a perfect setup. Most of the time I knew your schedule. I was just supposed to follow you and report. I felt like a spy in the movies. I also felt lousy."

"Which owners?" Scott asked.

"I wasn't always sure. Just a few of them, I think. I never met one."

"Who'd you work through?"

"Borini and Faslo."

"What!" Scott bunched his fists.

"They told me they thought you coming to hire them was pretty funny."

"I get this week's 'stupid' award. I shouldn't have hired anybody."

"You didn't know," I said.

Morty said, "They have a tap on your phone and a listening device in your living room. That's why it was so easy to keep track of you guys."

It chilled me to realize that our most intimate conversations may have been overheard. My anger increased, but I managed to ask, "How could they have a listening device?"

"I did it one day when I came over early last season."

I said, "You're responsible for the note in the hospital?"

He hung his head. "Yeah."

"When did you have a chance?" Scott asked.

"You were talking to a nurse for a few minutes. It only took a couple seconds to put it there."

I asked, "Did you or they blow up my truck?"

"I sure didn't. They never approved actual physical violence. They never did with me anyway. Maybe a couple of them were hoping somebody would just shoot you. It was more mischief than malice."

"Mischief?" I wanted to throttle the blithering dolt. How dare he attempt to minimize what to us had been months of terror? I felt Scott's hand on my arm. It was an unwelcome calming and soothing gesture. It was also effective. I subsided. I asked Scott, "How can you be so calm? You've been betrayed by a friend."

"Because I know it's going to be over." Scott asked Morty, "Was that you on the street who threatened me at the scene of the explosion?"

"No. That must have been one of their regular operatives. I had to be ready to go when and where they wanted me. They didn't use me a lot in the off-season. They called me earlier today. I had to hurry over until one of the regulars could show up. They wouldn't let me off the hook in the off-season. If I was needed, I had to go. They paid me a lot of money and made a lot of promises."

Scott asked, "Who tried to run us over on the North Side?"

"If it was a black Mercedes, it was one of their younger operatives, Lyle, Kyle, something. He gets a kick out of doing mean tricks. I heard him laughing about it. He thought you were funny as you jumped out of the way. I would never have done that."

Scott asked, "I've been followed all this time and my security people didn't notice them?"

"These guys are really good, but I don't think they meant you any real harm. Nobody was going to shoot you."

"How do you know that?" I asked.

"They promised me." Morty had been talking with his face pointed toward the ground. Now he looked up. Tears formed tiny rivulets on his porcine face. "I'm sorry. Especially about that note in the hospital. I'm really sorry. I had to. I would have been finished in baseball. I swear. You know I'm not that good."

"Were you the only one of the team they approached?" Scott asked.

"No one else ever spoke about it to me. Borini and Faslo never said there was. I had a career and my wife and kids to think about."

"What exactly were you supposed to do?" I asked.

"I was supposed to spy on you, like I was today. My duties were mostly on the team's road trips. With the explosion and all, it was a natural that I go to the hospital. I wanted to, understand, but they made me bring the note."

I asked, "What if you didn't have a chance to leave the note?"

"Then I would try something else. God, I feel awful. I feel like such a rat. I've never turned on a guy. Never. They put me in such a tough spot. What could I do?"

"You could have come to me," Scott said. "I'd have helped."

"You couldn't make me a better player. You couldn't have saved my career."

"Did you have anything to do with the clinic bombing?" I asked.

"Jesus, God, no!" Morty looked at me in horror. "You don't think I would do anything like that? Kill all those people? I don't hate you guys. I for sure don't care about abortion. I just wanted to play baseball."

I asked, "Did Borini and Faslo have anything to do with the explosion?"

"Not that I know of. They sure never talked to me about it."

Scott and I looked at each other. I said, "I think we need to pay a visit to Borini and Faslo."

"I think we need to plan and be organized," Scott said.

"You're really going over there?" Morty asked. "Maybe they'll just deny what's been going on. Then I'd be hung out to dry. I've got nothing in writing. I'm not even sure why you'd believe me."

"I'm not usually into conspiracies," I said. "At least not big, evil governmental ones, but I'm willing to buy this one."

Scott said, "I can believe some of the owners would be behind this."

Morty said, "I'll do what I can to make it up to you."

"A press conference," I said, "now, before they find out we know. Before they have time to organize damage control."

"What does that accomplish?" Scott asked. "We can't prove anything. They don't know there's damage to control, yet."

I was frustrated with Scott. "What good is caution going to do now? We've identified the bad guys."

"It wasn't some evil cabal of right-wing nuts," Scott said. "These are rich men."

"The country-club set has just as many right-wing nuts as anybody," I said, "maybe more."

"We should talk to a lawyer," Scott said. "We should talk to the police. We don't have any proof beyond what Morty says."

"I'm not lying," Morty said. "I feel awful about what I did. I'll do whatever you guys ask."

"This would give Kearn the scoop he needs," I said. "We haven't been able to give him much. He'll owe us. He'll get his face back on national television. The right-wing conspiracy unmasked."

"How is melodramatic posturing going to help us now?" Scott asked.

"I admit it," I said. "I am going over the top. I think it's justified. I'm elated. I'm ecstatic. This is our chance to stop a whole lot of crap. I want to make as big a splash as possible. You can be calm and reasonable. I'm not feeling that way. I want to get even in huge front-page headlines from coast to coast, and I think it will get headlines, great, big, splashy headlines that will put a stop to what's been happening to us."

Scott shook his head. "We need to think and plan. If we hold a press conference, they just deny everything. We need proof."

We both hate it when we disagree in front of others. I used to think of it as hypocrisy when my parents put on their party faces in front of company. Morty hardly rated as company since he was the resident traitor. Still I didn't want to continue arguing in front of him. We walked a few paces off, keeping ourselves between him and the shore end of the pier.

Scott said, "This is our chance to have the moral high ground. A real conspiracy, by at least some of the asshole owners." Scott loves to talk about seizing the moral high ground. I'm not sure being morally superior is all that it's cracked up to be. Say you've got a monopoly on truth and beauty. And if you're really well connected, you might have a hot line to whoever or whatever you consider to be God. The next guy can claim the same thing with as much authority. It's like the Bible being divinely inspired. Who said so? Some guy who claimed a direct link to God. With that many direct links, maybe God hires out, and instead of connecting with God, one day somebody got a secretary and not the genuine entity. I don't see the rise of righteousness in this country as a sign that Christianity has grown or that anyone is more morally superior.

I said, "I don't care about moral superiority. What difference does it make? I want the fear to stop."

"Tom?" Scott put all he could of the annoyed thrum of his deepest voice into that one syllable. It was his call for me to be reasonable. Calm. I'd been getting ridiculous and out of control. I needed to be sensible and rational. Plotting and conniving cleverly wouldn't be bad either.

I took a deep breath. "Do you have a plan?"

"The obvious way to get proof would be to have them on tape talking to Morty."

"We send him back to Borini and Faslo?"

"What they've done has got to be criminal. He could try to get them to admit something incriminating."

"Does that ever work outside the movies?"

"We can try. We can stage a dramatic, accusatory press conference if this doesn't work. For now, we could contact Pulver."

I said, "Okay. This is great. We'll need less protection now that we know the source of the attacks."

"Are you sure we need less protection?"

"Double conspiracies? Borini, Faslo, and McCutcheon? Even the most hardened nutcase would find that hard to swallow. I'm not ready to think they could plan that massively, that every protection we've tried has been tainted with our enemies." I hesitated. I was sure of that, wasn't I?

Scott said, "We've got to go with what we've got. Pulver must know people with access to taping equipment."

It wasn't hard getting hold of Pulver. He could help us, but there was a lot more red tape than I thought. On television, don't they just pull the taping equipment out of a drawer and go to work? Seems that way. We set up a meeting in the Twenty-third District police station at Halsted and Addison, just three blocks from Wrigley Field. Morty accompanied us. Every few minutes he apologized. He looked like a mortally wounded bear ready to bawl at the slightest provocation. He kept promising to make it up to us.

Pulver called in his superiors and a state's attorney. Once officials began to assemble, help began to happen quickly. I knew with this many people involved there was no way we would keep it out of the media. That was fine with me. I'd come over to Scott's side that we needed to get more proof, but I was ready to do some denouncing from as many podiums as I could mount. Scott says when I get like that, I need a good slap upside the head. I do tend to get overdramatic, and I love cheap sentiment.

It only took a couple hours to set it all up. Pulver told us we were lucky. They were eager to cooperate for several reasons: Scott's fame, the possibility of lots of good publicity for the cops, and a possible career-making moment for the state's attorney if all of this proved to be true. Plus, several of Pulver's superiors were eager to take Borini and Faslo down. They'd been burned in court by that firm and would be happy to see huge headlines with pictures of them being hauled away in chains. I'm not the only one on earth who can be overly dramatic.

In a lull while we were waiting, I asked Pulver if he knew anything about Myrtle Mae's interview with the police.

"Who?" he asked.

"A drag queen whose real name was Bryce Bennet."

"Oh, I heard. They didn't know he was a drag queen when he first came in. When the cops arrived to question him, he was wearing a very expensive suit. He didn't seem to know anything."

From long experience, Myrtle Mae wore his most conservative outfits when dealing with the police. He may have been an outrageous queen, but he wasn't stupid. We'd asked Pulver to find out why the police were going to be questioning Myrtle Mae again.

Morty had demanded and gotten an appointment with Borini and Faslo for late that afternoon. We were permitted to sit in the back of a police car and stay out of the way. Only Jessica Fletcher gets to do the good stuff. In reality we were lucky to get that much.

The state's attorney practiced with Morty before he went up. He told Morty which things he had to try to get them to say. "Insist that you have to meet with the owners," the state's attorney said. Morty agreed to everything. He practiced his lines numerous times, like a high school jock who was in the school play for the first time. Typecast once again.

▲ 25 ▲

Being in the back of a police car was odd. There really were no handles for the doors or windows. We weren't going to get out unless somebody let us out. I don't think we were particularly recognizable, but people craned their necks in that I'm-not-really-looking-I-just-happen-to-walk-in-this-nearly-hunched-over-way-staring-into-the-backseat-of-parked-cop-cars look. The surveillance van with the bugging equipment was almost out of sight around a corner.

We were sitting on Wells Street under the el tracks a couple blocks from Sears Tower. While we sat, the uniformed cop who drove us walked over to a deli across the street and ate a sub sandwich at the counter. I hoped he didn't decide to go far. I didn't want to be stuck in the backseat with no possible exit and no person around to let us out.

In the back of the cop car, for the first time in hours I had time to reflect. Giddy relief at the end of our fear mixed with the residue of our argument.

"I shouldn't have walked out," Scott said. "How is that supposed to help?"

"I push too hard. I don't listen." I joined the orgy of apology. "I feel rotten. I'd have been really upset if you'd been hurt."

"I made an adult decision. It was my choice. Not a very good one. I just had to get away for a few minutes. I was coming back."

"I always want you to come back. I always want to be there when you do." We held hands in the backseat of the car for a while.

Half an hour later, we got the cop to let us out so we could get ourselves some coffee and sandwiches at the deli. Finally, after two hours, the state's attorney walked up to where we were leaning our butts against the car.

"Did you get what you needed?" I asked.

"Yes. A surprisingly nasty amount. Your buddy did a great job. That, and Mr. Faslo has a tendency to brag."

"What did Morty do?" I asked.

"Played his script perfectly. He asked for a meeting with some of the owners. Demanded a guaranteed contract with a specific minor league team with a clause to move him up to the majors in five years. For such a high-powered firm, they were pathetically vulnerable to someone like Morty turning on them. They tried threatening him and weaseling around, but he's got a stolid doggedness that worked better than any threats or bluster. He was pretty persuasive. We owe him some."

I said, "He owed us a great deal to begin with."

"I guess you're right," the state's attorney said.

Clayton Pulver drove up in a white 1965 Rambler. The car seemed totally out of place for Pulver. With him was Morty.

The first words Morty said to us were "I'm sorry." They

were also the last and most of the words in the middle. I appreciated the sentiment, but I wasn't ready to forgive yet. I remembered all too clearly the hurt and the fear we'd been through.

"What happened?" Scott asked him.

"They kept reassuring me," Morty said. "I talked about how scared I was after the bombing. I said you'd nearly caught me today. I just pushed until they called one of the owners and got him on the phone. It was great."

"Did you get the phone conversation taped?" I asked.

"It wasn't necessary," the state's attorney said. "We have plenty without it."

"Now what?" I asked.

The state's attorney said, "We hold a press conference. They don't know what we've got. We want to use the element of surprise on them."

"Isn't that kind of quick?" Scott asked.

"You want the threats to stop?" Pulver asked.

I said immediately, "Definitely."

We arranged for Brandon Kearn to get an interview before the press conference. He and his station got an exclusive for half an hour. I don't understand why getting the scoop is so important these days. It seems as if every media outlet spends hours beating to death every single detail of even the most insignificant story. After the overkill and often useless live reports, they trot out the talking heads. That whole shtick never makes sense to me. But then I think talk radio is a lot of moronic blather led by and fed by people who desperately need to get a life. But people are paying attention to them. It's hard for me to imagine anything dumber than setting policy because of comments made on talk radio.

When I called, Kearn explained that he'd been interviewing the survivors who lived in the same building as Thornburg. He'd been unable to interview Omega Collins as he was hot on the scent, often finding people before the police did. It was still not definite that Thornburg had set off the explosion.

On the way to the interview, Scott and I agreed we could drop McCutcheon and his services or at least go back to using him and his company only for public appearances. At least until we were able to hire a new one. I had the pleasure of giving McCutcheon the news.

McCutcheon and I spoke in the corridor outside the room where the press conference was being held. Besides telling him about the cutbacks, I asked, "How come you never noticed these guys following Scott around?"

He shrugged. "It was a teammate. Someone he trusted implicitly. Scott confided in him about his schedule or casually mentioned where he might be going. Hiding something, or in this case someone, out in the open is always preferable when you can do it. Remember, my firm is mostly designed for public events. No one thought you needed round-the-clock protection until this whole latest mess began. I'm glad you found who did it. I wish I had found them first. I'm going to be sorry not to be working for you guys."

I felt like kind of a heel since he wasn't the guilty party.

We also called our lawyer to discuss a possible lawsuit against the owners and Borini and Faslo.

"Possible?" he asked. "After we're through with them, you'll be able to buy a small country."

Kearn was nearly as grateful as Morty was apologetic. Two hours later as the news conference was breaking up, I asked Kearn if he had any more news on the bombing or on Myrtle Mae. He didn't.

"I'm going to go over the tapes again when I get home," I

234

said. "There's got to be a clue there. Myrtle Mae was no dummy. He saw something on those tapes. I'm sure of it. Someone who doesn't belong or something that is out of whack."

"You're sure he said it was on the tapes?" Kearn asked.

"That's what his message said."

"I've got something else for you. I have it on good authority that the Tools of Satan terrorist group was in fact a real organization. That they did have an office in a building across the alley. It is possible that some of the workers in that organization were bringing in a bomb to use, and it blew up prematurely. Or someone could have been trying to bomb them."

"Why take out the whole damn block?" I asked.

"Getting a huge impact is at least as important as setting the bomb in the first place. Or it could have been supplies that went off accidentally. Rumors are starting that they could have been planning to bomb that banquet of protesters, but they blew themselves up."

"That sounds like a crock."

Kearn shrugged. "You'd like it to be about your friends or your causes because then it makes more sense to you. But it doesn't have to be about you or the clinic. Chaos happens and innocent people are caught in the middle of it."

We decided to drive over to our penthouse for the tapes. I wouldn't feel comfortable about staying there until we had debugging experts comb the place thoroughly. We could watch the tapes and be careful what we said. Better yet we could take them to my place out in the country. Morty had told us where the one bug he planted was, but we weren't going to take any chances. Kearn would follow us. Our lawyer was already working with the phone company and the police about the illegal tap on our line.

In the car Scott asked, "Are we going to give up the notion of finding out who the bombers were?"

"I guess I would, but I'm wondering who killed Myrtle Mae. Why would he be dead? Why would he give us a message about looking at those tapes? He didn't see them."

"I don't think we're ever going to discover who did either one," Scott said. "We've got the weekend still to get away. I know it's not a lead-lined bunker, but I could hire a jet and we could get away for a day or two. You're not due back to work until Monday."

"And I have my doctor's note to prove my illness." I still experienced a little dizziness at times, and I was often tired. I figured a few more days of rest and I would be ready to face the hordes of teenagers in my classroom. Going back after a sub has had your class for a week can be a hassle. Even the best substitutes usually manage to mess things up.

As we ascended in the elevator to the penthouse, I said, "Before we go to my place I think I'm going to look at those tapes one more time. If Myrtle Mae thought there was something odd about them, then there has to be."

Scott said, "If we're going to be at your place, I want to take a few tools and some lumber with me."

The quiet in the penthouse was broken only by the hum of distant appliances. We found the bugging device Morty had mentioned. I wanted to take one of Scott's hammers and smash it into smithereens, but it was evidence. A cop and a state's attorney met us to do a preliminary search of the apartment. They took it away with them.

Kearn followed me to the electronics room. "I may not be able to let you keep these," he said. "The station is getting anxious to make sure everything connected with the case is accounted for."

"What's the big deal?" I asked. "We've only got copies."

"I wonder what it was that Bryce Bennet saw? I want to look through these again myself."

"He watched the overnight news. It was a joke among his friends." A thought struck me. "Maybe he didn't want the tapes of the event. Maybe he wanted the tapes of the coverage. What exactly did he say on his message?" I couldn't remember.

"The coverage on the news?" Kearn asked.

"Or maybe he wanted to compare the two. He must have been onto something."

"I'm inclined to Scott's position that Bryce Bennet didn't have a clue."

Hearing Myrtle Mae referred to by his real name always startled me, doubly so with the repetition. "Who was your source in the department about what Myrtle Mae knew?"

"Your source in the department couldn't tell you?"

"I'm not going to start playing games. I was kind of wondering who told you he was a drag queen."

"Beg pardon?"

"You used the name Bryce Bennet when you met us outside his apartment, but when we saw the body, you made a crack about him being a drag queen. How did you know that?"

"I was told at the police station."

"But Myrtle Mae wasn't in drag. Pulver told us he'd shown up in a business suit. No one would have known."

"It was general knowledge."

"Which you didn't have. I had to tell you."

That's when Kearn pulled out a gun.

"Myrtle Mae saw something on the tapes," I said. "He knew you were guilty of something."

"From my contacts with the police, I knew Bryce Bennet was onto something. It wasn't the tapes, not then. The initial problem was I heard Bennet knew something that had to do with the Fattatuchis' kid. Maybe Bennet had gotten to him. The Fattatuchi kid was a militia wanna-be. He was suspicious about the truth. He was Thornburg's contact. He was helping to hide him. We managed to kill both of them. Turns out activists in Chicago were hiding Thornburg."

"What did Myrtle Mae know specifically? Why did he have to die?"

"What did the drag queen know and when did he know it?" Kearn laughed. "Do you really care about one dead drag queen?"

Thoughts of physically harming the handsome menace flashed through my mind. The gun in his hand was argument enough to prevent the thought from becoming an action. I said, "He was a good friend."

"He was a neurotic busybody sticking his nose in where it didn't belong. Sort of like yourself."

"Thornburg and Fattatuchi were dead. What was the problem?"

"We didn't know who else the Fattatuchi kid might have told. Myrtle Mae's knowledge probably wouldn't have led to anything, but we couldn't be sure."

"Did the Fattatuchi kid confide in Myrtle Mae?"

"I tried to find out. Bennet wouldn't tell. The possibility that he knew something was a threat to me—he had to die. I knew he was a drag queen because when I showed up to find out what he knew, he conducted the interview as he dressed. He may have been going to wear a business suit to see the cops, but I had to watch him in his dressing room primping more assiduously than an expensive whore."

Myrtle Mae loved to chat as he "pulled himself together." He transacted a lot of gay rights negotiations over his vats of makeup.

"The guy bragged incessantly that 'no one is going to pull the chiffon over the eyes of this drag queen.' "

That was one of Myrtle Mae's favorite twists on a cliché. "You had to get rid of him because he could identify you as the bomber?"

The gun didn't waver and nothing loud or dramatic happened. "Pretty much. The son of a bitch was suspicious."

"Why do the bombing in the first place?"

"Two reasons. Braxton Thornburg was ready to turn us in. He was going to try and work a deal with the authorities. He would give evidence of our group if the government would go easy on him."

"How do you know he hadn't already told? If he was negotiating, how come he wasn't arrested?"

"His lawyer was negotiating. I have sources. I knew I hadn't been named yet. I was worried about what he might tell his lawyer. The clinic was conveniently across the alley as a cover for the real crime."

"But why kill all those people?"

"Who would think of a terrorist bombing being used as a cover for a murder of someone who was in the way?"

"But what did he know about you? What had you done that was illegal?"

"Other terrorist bombings and shootings. The last two smaller-scale bombs that had been left killed a few people here and there. We did those. The underground network knew that. There is a secret, violent underground network. When rumors surfaced that Thornburg was going to testify, he had to be stopped. We decided we could kill him and make a statement. Nobody would dare betray us again."

"There's an international conspiracy to blow up abortion clinics?"

"Not so much of a conspiracy as a loosely knit group of people who cooperate with each other. My main camera guy and I were in it together."

"How'd you know how to put a bomb together?"

"Really, who has to know that nowadays? You just connect to the Internet and bippiddy, boppiddy, boo, you've got a bomb."

"Why did you do so much investigating? Why did you keep getting us involved?"

"Because I intended to keep being a reporter. My job is a fabulous cover. I had to milk this story for all it was worth. You guys as an interview would have been great. Keeping an eye on what you knew was even better. I doubted if you'd find out anything, but I couldn't be sure. What was even more perfect, the more I uncovered, the better I could scatter suspicion in every direction."

"What was the deal with the tapes?"

"What Bennet told me, before I killed him, was that he was watching late-night local-television news and saw our report on that protest in the north suburbs. He knew the priest who got hurt. He saw our interview with him. Bennet didn't think we had time to get back for the bombing. He thought we arrived too soon. That we couldn't have gotten from the far North Side to the scene in the time it said. The timing display on the tape was supposedly a giveaway. He was wrong. Scott was right. Bennet had screwed it up. Unfortunately, he could alert half the planet to a possible anomaly."

"If there was no problem with the tapes, why come back here to get them?"

"The tough part was, we did have a real problem. Somebody needed extra tapes at the scene. They simply came to our truck and took them. My cameraman left used tapes in what he thought was a secure place, but reporters were desperate that night. Nobody'd ever used that much tape. There were more than a zillion cameras. They took every tape that wasn't nailed down. Only later did we realize we had made a mistake. See, we'd taped ourselves setting the bomb."

"Home movies of the crazed and conscienceless."

"When he realized the mistake, it was too late. Our truck had been caught in the secondary explosion. We were a little careless then. We didn't think the second bomb would be that powerful. We couldn't find the tape of ourselves. When we couldn't find it, we believed it had gone up with the van. We figured we were safe. The station made all those copies for you. There are an incredible number of hours of tape of what happened. We discovered a few brief snippets of ourselves on one of the tapes. Most of it had been taped over, but not everything. We destroyed the original. We got the copy from the cops. That's where I was when I didn't answer my pager this morning. We still had to get yours. You have that bit. None of them had noticed the oddity. It's only for a few seconds at the beginning. Shown frame by frame it is off-kilter. It isn't much, but it could be fatal. Until you offered to come back here, we thought we'd have to kill you both. I thought that would be kind of a shame, because I kind of like you both. Unfortunately, you caught my slip about Bennet."

"When we met you outside his building, you'd just killed him."

"Yes. I was forced to use one of the oldest tricks in the book. I spotted you trying to find a parking place. Instead of running, I turned around and made it look as if I was just arriving as well."

"If Myrtle Mae thought you were the killer, why'd he let you in?"

"He was suspicious, but he wasn't sure. He thought he'd get me to slip up. He wasn't as clever as he thought he was."

"Maybe you aren't either. People know the three of us came here together."

"I appreciate your concern about my getting away with this, but you needn't worry. You'll be dead."

I worried about where Scott was and how I could warn him to stay away, get out, call the police, and rescue us.

"Why did you set the bomb off that night?"

"Thornburg might be going to cooperate. He also could skip town. We had to act quickly. With that banquet of protesters in town, it was perfect. I figured I could put suspicion on a lot of people. I had a contact at the convention in Wisconsin. When I found out that Clancey was coming to town, I figured this would be a great day to strike.

"My main problem during the investigation was holding back on the knowledge I had. I couldn't be seen to know too much too soon. I *had* to look like I was investigating. You guys actually helped there. It would have been a perfect murder if it hadn't been for that goddamn drag queen."

"Why did you blow up my truck?"

"That was fortuitous chance. We wanted one more little explosion to round everything off. We wanted to divert suspicion completely. I recognized the truck from an interview I did with Scott from before he came out. I saw you guys drive off in it together. When I saw it in the clinic parking lot, I thought it would be perfect. What greater way to divert suspicion from our real purpose?"

Scott walked into the room carrying a six-foot-long, two-inch-thick wooden plank on his shoulder. He held it in such a way that Kearn was not in his line of vision.

"Have you been messing with my tools?"

I am never to touch Scott's tools. He told me he'd get me my own set. I promised and promised to put things back exactly where I found them. He told me it was like how I wanted my own newspaper every day. That I didn't want sections that he'd read through. I know my peccadillo doesn't make much sense, but neither does his. But it was one of those compromises. And I don't need tools all that often. And what was the point of hassling each other about something we could both afford?

Kearn swung his gun in Scott's direction and commanded, "Put the board down." He began advancing toward Scott.

Scott looked at me and knew I hadn't spoken. He swung the board around to look for the other voice. He caught Kearn in the solar plexus. The reporter doubled over. The gun fired. The bullet thunked into the wood, passed through, and tore a tunnel through the carpet. Scott bashed him one on the head.

Kearn crumpled to the floor.

I said, "He's the bomber."

"Kearn? How do you know?"

"Myrtle Mae was right and wrong." I explained about the Fattatuchis' son, the tapes, and Kearn's excess of knowledge about Myrtle Mae.

"He killed all those people just to do away with a rival terrorist?"

"It would have been a perfect murder. His cameraman was also one of the fanatic antiabortionists. They worked together."

While waiting for the police, we trussed Kearn up and tied him to a kitchen chair. When he came around, Scott asked,

"Don't you feel guilty about killing all those people?"

"Guilt? No, I let the good Christians do guilt."

Pulver showed up with McCutcheon about twenty minutes later. Jantoro arrived soon after. He brought several beat cops with him.

We explained everything. Kearn didn't say a word to the cops. They took him away along with the tapes. I felt incredible relief that all the crap was finally going to be over. We refused to be part of the press conference that was held to announce the capture of the bomber. I'd had enough of that for a lifetime. Scott agreed.

Before heading out to my place that night, we visited the hospital. In Alan Redpath's room Oliver was asleep in the chair. I stood next to Alan. Except for an IV connection to his arm, he was no longer hooked up to any machines. I found the nurse and asked her how he was. She said that he was out of danger and would recover. I returned to the room. Scott and a sleepy Oliver were talking softly. I saw Alan open his eyes. He smiled groggily and reached out his arms to me. I picked him up and held him. I hoped he found as much comfort and satisfaction as I did as his small arms reached around my neck and shoulder.

Over the next few days and weeks several things happened. First, we decided on a simple trip to our cabin in northern Wisconsin as a break for the weekend.

They investigated for weeks, but Kearn's vast network of a conspiracy turned up only two more people, besides the cameraman.

We were talking with Pulver and McCutcheon one night

after one of Scott's appearances. We hadn't hired a new firm yet.

Pulver said, "It's hard to tell with these conspiracy folks. Their numbers get larger the more vivid their imaginations. I think their power and influence is greatly exaggerated."

The lawsuit against Borini and Faslo and three baseball team owners they were working for never got to court. Borini and Faslo were bankrupted because of the settlement, but the owners had to pay. We didn't buy a small country. We did get a minor league franchise in Chicago's south suburbs. We added the cash from the settlement to what we got in reward for catching the bomber and set up a trust fund for the kids hurt in the blast.

The day we solved the mystery, we went to my place in the country. Mostly I sat and stared at the flat countryside around my home. I listened to tapes of Judy Collins. Scott worked for a while on another carpentry project.

That night we lay awake together in my bed in each other's arms. I listened to the last insects of fall and the soft breeze through the window, which was open to the last warmth of the summer. I still couldn't fall asleep. I always wanted my life to have made a difference to the world. I know you can only change the little part that is close to you, and even that part not all that often. Perhaps I've always thought my life would be justified if I at least added a little kindness to the world. I know most of us are less than a blip in the vast history of the universe, but I think most of us like to think we'll have some kind of immortality beyond that which is promised but unproved by most major religions.

I felt Scott's arms sag and his head lean against mine. His breathing became more regular. If there was to be comfort in the world, this was about as much as I or anybody else would ever get. Love for a good person who in turn loved me.

I stayed in that position until my arm fell asleep. Then I eased it carefully out from under him. I lay in bed and stared at the ceiling trying to think of anything but being blown up. But memories do fade and sleep does come and we do move on, and we are not paralyzed by a universe too unimaginably vast to comprehend.